Clash by Night

I0521382

Other people's dreams ...

Joseph McConnell

ProcArch LLC, Ann Arbor

ISBN: 978-0-9963385-0-9

First edition, 2013.

The headings are from the poem <u>Dover Beach</u>, written in 1851 by Matthew Arnold. Together with Yeats' <u>The Second Coming</u>, it surely must stand as one of the most prescient works of poetry in English.

This is a work of fiction. All characters in this work are fictional, and they do not represent real people. The Ann Arbor Police Department, the FBI, the CIA, and the University of Michigan's History Department do not have personnel such as those described here, nor are the procedural details necessarily accurate. There is no such city as Gardner, Michigan. Although there is a Sturgis and a Sturgis Police Department, the officers depicted here have no basis in reality, nor do police departments take such a casual approach to retiring their working dogs as the plot of this book would suggest.

Ann Arbor actually has three separate art fairs, all of which take place during the same week each year. That week is in July, not June, and the author pleads poetic license in bringing it forward a month.

This book is for Linda and for all the Old Towners and Technocrats who make this strange little burg worth living in. Thanks to Dennis Baer for Air Force lore.

The sea is calm tonight ...

June weather napped the city in a green haze, like a dish in *salsa verde*. Lockwood Street on Ann Arbor's southeast side was a bit more suburban-feeling than other parts of town. It was built up in the Eighties, partly by developers, partly by individual homeowners. Thirty-some years later, its five blocks between Packard and Independence were now occupied by a Volvo-and-Prius demographic, no longer by the BMW and Mercedes owners for whom the homes had been built. Don Perry's house was in the middle of one of those blocks, and his trash, recycling, and compost bins were sitting out by the curb along with those of his neighbors. Tonight, though, Don's plastic dumpsters had been joined by a foreign object, a box or something, three feet square, light tan in the very late evening sun.

Don parked his Escort (he was a Ford employee with a long and unaesthetic commute) and examined the thing someone had left for him. Up close, it seemed to be a rectangular frame covered with a tightly-stretched heavy cloth, probably canvas. There weren't any markings or labels, but on each of the four vertical sides, there was a small hole, stained with black. And on the top, there were reddish smudges that looked a great deal like blood.

Four blocks away, a small dinner party was going on. Not everyone would calculate the count of dinner guests and include non-human beings, but not everyone, not many people, in fact, had the same attitude toward things as Mac MacArthur. This particular evening, Mac had cooked for four, but planned on entertaining six: four bipeds and two quads. His human friends were seated around the dinner table, and the two resident German Shepherds, Snacker and Goose, were under it. Snacker had seniority—she was elderly, gray around the muzzle, and clearly in charge of the canine administrative unit. As a pound dog, her ancestry was a bit uncertain, but the bulk of it was German Shepherd, for sure. The rest might have been snow dog or even Labrador; regardless, she was *dog* only in the eyes of others. In her own mind, she was an adult member of the family, Director of Security for the pack, and always, always, underfed.

Goose was a more recent recruit. He and Mac had become acquainted a year before, when they were part of an ad hoc law enforcement team that found itself inadvertently in a confused and unnecessary shootout.

1

Goose did well, acting in his capacity as a canine officer of the Sturgis, Michigan police department. Afterward, there had been quite a bit of standing around while a vast number of federal agents scurried about, and Goose and Mac had established a certain rapport.

Not too long after that, Mac got a call from the Sturgis officer responsible for Goose. Goose, it seemed, had decided to take early retirement. He no longer wanted to go out and find people, bad guys or otherwise; he was reluctant even to get in the patrol car, let alone get out again at crime scenes; and he was generally exhibiting signs of boredom with the whole chase-'em-and-bite-'em job description. Since his handler already had one retired police dog on his hands, plus a human child on the way, he wasn't ready to take on another retiree. The gist of the call to Mac was, you two seemed to get along; would you be able to take Goose off our hands?

The implied comparison between Mac and Goose—that they'd make a good match—wasn't lost on MacArthur. He himself was a retiree, unwillingly but effectively. Cancer, of a kind described as treatable but not curable, had put him on the sidelines, benched him from his job as an Ann Arbor police detective, and left him with time on his hands. He didn't think the Sturgis officer was really saying anything derogatory (although the man *had* been present when Mac emptied a pistol at an armed adversary twenty feet away and hit nothing but trees and dirt.) Mac remembered Goose as a pleasant, slightly aloof dog and was inclined to say yes, but not without getting agreement from the other stakeholders, Snacker and of course, Mac's wife, Colleen. She certainly got a say in the matter, since these days she was the alpha human, what with Mac being officially and to a great extent actually retired.

So there was a trip to Sturgis, over toward Michigan's west side. Snacker and Goose exchanged sniffs and then play-bows, the manic gesture between dogs that means, "Let's romp!' or "Chase me!", and the deal was basically done; Colleen wasn't good at denying Snacker anything she wanted. Months later, Goose was just another member of the family, ranking fourth and not seeming to mind at all. For one thing, the chow hall was better than in his last posting, since here dogs weren't banned from the kitchen (or anywhere else, for that matter.) In fact, since Mac was stiff and creaky in his joints and unenthusiastic about bending down, the dogs were actually encouraged to hang around and clean up anything that might hit the floor, short of entire portions.

From closely observing Snacker and her interaction with Mac and Colleen, Goose picked up the MacArthur household dialect. When humans said "snacks" or "treats," it meant eating was going on or about to be. "Biscuit" was a synonym. "Go see ..." followed by a person's name, meant go find Mac or Colleen, usually indicating that a car ride or a walk was n the cards. When speaking in Shepherd, one short bark was a magic incantation that would cause a human to appear, open the back door wall, and let a dog or dogs in from the yard. Of course, if you were already in, the bark could mean "out" or some other contextually obvious request. And if there was some urgency about it, you could prefix it slightly, making it more of a "Ga-wuff," than just a "Wuff." Non-verbally, there were techniques for pointing; humans would extend a finger in the direction of something interesting, like a fallen food item or a squirrel, whereas dogs would make eye contact, then look at the desired object, usually the back door or a food item (fallen or not.) The usual shared language terms, "Sit," "Stay," "Down," and so on, Goose already knew. There were some other words he knew, in English and German, but Mac and Colleen were careful not to use them, and they were gradually slipping from Goose's memory.

The humans around the table, besides Mac and Colleen, were two more of the participants in that Sturgis gunfight event, Jenn Langton and Andy Patel. Jenn was an Ann Arbor detective, a woman Mac had helped train. Andy was an FBI agent from the Detroit office, an ex-Marine, getting to be a friend of Mac's and lately, apparently, something more than a friend of Jenn's. Tonight's gathering was the second time the four of them had dined together, and Mac and Colleen were curious about the nature and extent of things. Could this be an actual relationship? There was a great deal of deduction going on, beneath the shop talk and griping about road construction. Mac noted that they arrived in one car, at the very least meaning that one of them had picked the other one up. No public displays of affection were in evidence yet, but—was that a knowing glance they'd just exchanged? It was all light and amusing, an older couple who knew each other very, very well, getting to know what might be in the process of becoming a younger couple. Under the table, the dogs yawned and stretched.

It had been an early dinner in deference to Andy's drive back into the Detroit suburbs. They were finished with everything except the cheese plate when Mac's cell phone went off. He looked at the display: "Huh. It's Don. Wonder what's on his mind?" He walked out into the kitchen and answered the call. The other three could hear his side of the conversation.

"Yeah, Don."

"Say that again."

"Sitting out with your trash bins?"

"Well, did you call the cops?"

"Don, I'm not a cop anymore ... I have a house full of them right now, but ..."

"Bullet holes and blood?!"

"Hold on a second."

Mac went back to the dining room.

"Would you folks like to go see something wacky? This is a friend of ours from a couple of blocks over that way." Mac pointed vaguely southwest. "Somebody left something weird out by his trash. Might actually be a crime of some kind."

As the streets ran in this rather unplanned part of town, Don's house was only half a mile away, but the four human diners still drove there, taking two cars. Mac was capable of walking that distance, but it would have taken a while, and he'd have been out of breath when they arrived. Standing up in the kitchen, making dinner, had been quite enough exercise already. Snacker and Goose were given a biscuit each and told to "hold the fort."

When they pulled up, Don Perry was standing by the street. His wife, Carol, was with him, having gotten home from her own north-suburbs job just in the last few minutes. They were old friends of the MacArthurs; Mac dealt with the introductions.

"Don, Carol, this is Jenn Langton. Unlike me, she's still really a cop. And this is Andy Patel. Although he tries to hide it, he's FBI."

"FBI?" said Don. "I didn't expect ..."

"Yeah, I know, the Spanish Inquisition. It's just social. Andy did some work with us last year, and we were reminiscing." It was some pretty good work, too, Mac thought. Andy and his proficiency with an M-14 had kept MacArthur from being seriously inconvenienced by a kid and a shotgun. That had been a strange day: a few moments of wild violence in the midst of a bizarre case, far outside the jurisdiction of the Ann Arbor Police Department. He doubted that the piece of volunteer trash Don had to show them (or anything else for that matter) would match the pure insanity of that gunfight in the countryside. As it turned out, he was wrong.

The "device" as it came to be called, was a cube with each side looking about a yard square. In fact, it measured *exactly* a yard in each dimension. The covering seemed to be sailcloth. The only structural difference among the sides was on the bottom; there, each corner rested on a dark metallic ball. They didn't seem to be rollers or castors, they were just feet. Mac took out his key ring and turned on the small flashlight he kept on it. Andy and Jenn gathered in as he looked quickly at the surfaces. The cloth on top was intact although stained. The bottom surface, of course, was invisible. But each of the vertical sides had, as Don had said on the phone, a small, centered hole, a little more than a quarter of an inch across. The cloth edges were slightly ragged, and around each of the holes, there was a black stain. Perhaps smudge would be a better word.

Andy said, "Do those look like bullet entries to you?"

Mac said, "Maybe. The stains look darker that I'd expect, though."

Jenn bent down and turned her own flashlight on one of the holes. "I don't know if I'd call that an *entry*. Look at the fibers."

The threads from the canvas or whatever material it was did, when you looked closely, seem to have been thrust out from the surface, not inward.

"Are they through-and-through? You know, in one side and out the other?" asked Mac.

"Doesn't look like it," said Jenn, moving around to the opposite side. "This one's the same. Fibers outwards."

Andy stood up abruptly and stepped back. "You know, I don't think we ought to mess with this thing. If those *are* shot holes ..."

Mac said, "... and if they came from *inside* it ..."

Everybody backed off. Colleen, Don, and Carol backed off further. The three cops looked at each other, and Mac stepped carefully back toward the device. Groaning slightly, he got down on his knees and pointed his tiny light into the nearest of the holes, holding it back about a foot and off to the side. Trying to keep his body aligned with an edge rather than a side of the box, he bent forward and looked through the hole.

"Jesus!" he said, and moved backwards, then accepted a hand up from Andy. "There's a pistol in there!"

... the turbid ebb and flow of human misery ...

In American schools, children hear about the Sioux and Apache and, perhaps, the Cherokee. In Canada, they hear about the Inuit and Inupiat. If they learn anything about native peoples and ethnicity and the callous disregard for cultures other than those of Western Europe, it's probably The Trail of Tears or Wounded Knee. Not many of our high school graduates recognize the names Igbo, Yoruba, or Hausa/Fulani.

And yet, more recently than the Custer fight or the campaigns against Geronimo, Great Britain and its economy mashed together a vast portion

6

of West Africa along and around the Niger River and called it Nigeria. There were and are hundreds of distinct ethnic groups in the resulting territory, and the Igbo, Yoruba, and Hausa/Fulani are the three largest. For fifty years, Britain ran Nigeria as a colony, with the Igbo east and the Yoruba west moving toward a form of cultural Europeanization, and the north retaining much more of its original structure. Ominously, the split also mirrored religious distinctions. Very broadly speaking, the north remained Islamic; the south and east became Christian or stayed Traditionalist.

In 1960, Nigeria became independent, and three years later it severed ties with Britain completely. An Igbo leader became its first president. In that same year, 1963, a young Igbo man from Port Harcourt in the southwest of Nigeria was in London, finishing a degree in economics. His name was Echezonachukwu Mbanugo; he made friends with the more left-leaning of his fellow students, and he told them to call him Jerry. His goal in being there was nothing more lofty than getting an English education and going home to join Nigeria's new elites, the government employees and what the Japanese would call the salarymen of the new Republic.

Then, on a smoggy London evening, he went alone to a pub in the East End. A friend was supposed to meet him, but that person never arrived. Instead, a young woman sat down and asked him where he came from. Instead of the caution and reserve that question might have produced (it usually did produce it, in fact,) her open and brightly curious manner charmed him. Her accent was a bit hard to identify, with its broad A and clipped pronunciation, and when it finally occurred to him to stop talking about himself and inquire about her, he discovered that she was an American. He'd never met one prior to that, his circle of acquaintances being limited to a few other Nigerian students and some British lefties. Over the next month, they saw each other several more times. Gradually, without it being really clear how, the gist of their conversations came to be: Jerry is homesick.

Once it had been said, either by Jerry or by his new friend, that Jerry was tired of London and would welcome a way to go home, if he could only be sure of employment once he got there, the next step was quick and predictable. The girl brought an acquaintance along to the pub, a Mr.

Adams, somewhat older, wearing a suit. And although he encouraged Jerry to stay in university and finish his degree, he talked about how that degree might not be a guarantee of anything, back in Port Harcourt or even Lagos. Things were not going too well for educated young men, he implied. Family was everything, connections were critical. If Jerry wanted to be sure of a job, he might want to consider a position with his, Mr. Adams', firm.

What that firm might be didn't immediately emerge. As it worked out, Jerry did manage to graduate, and when he did, he let Adams know that he was ready to talk in more detail. The detail was simple: he was to go back home, take the entry-level office position that was on offer, and from time to time look into things that he'd be asked to look into. Although the name was never pronounced, never even alluded to, the fact of the matter was that Jerry, along with eleven other young Nigerian students, had just been recruited by the CIA. At that point, Nigeria was just two years away from a series of coups and three years from a bloody civil war. There would be no overt US involvement, but the Western powers were getting their pawns aligned on the board.

... like a land of dreams ...

The crime scene on Lockwood Street came and went rapidly enough. Jenn Langton, being the only serving police officer with jurisdiction, got the task of calling headquarters and reporting a suspicious object. If ever there was a suspicious object, the device certainly qualified. It couldn't have been more suspicious if it had been labeled "Acme Bomb Company." Sniffer equipment confirmed that it contained gunpowder residue, or at least the chemical components of gunpowder. The stains on top would take longer to assess, but they looked like bloodstains to everybody who'd seen bloodstains before. Of course, being cops, the cops and ex-cops standing around in the spring evening started dreaming up explanations.

Ann Arbor's police chief Fredricks, dropping in on his way home, had questions about Don and Carol. Neither Mac, who'd known them for years, nor any neighbors could think of reasons why someone would leave them a suspicious object. Likewise, nobody could imagine why either of them would have built the thing, let alone abandon it post-use on their own sidewalk. Mac, watching the experts carefully lifting the device and putting it in a truck, was thinking along other lines.

"Seems to me like some kind of booby trap," he said, mostly to Jenn, partly to anyone else listening. "Maybe some kind of 'Keep off my lawn!' thing?"

Jenn made a noncommittal gesture, a wave-shrug motion involving both hands and a shoulder. "But if it went off and hit somebody, why don't we have a report?"

"Hospitals?" asked Mac. "Anybody go into ER today with a gunshot wound?"

"No, nothing in the last three days," said Jenn. "I checked. Not at the U, not at Saint Joe." The University of Michigan Health System and Saint Joseph Mercy Hospital were the two most likely places in the area for a badly-injured person to end up. She was doing the phone calls because she'd caught the case—been assigned to it—more or less by default, but also because she asked for it. The last time she'd had a strange crime to chase down, she'd fallen short of her own expectations, although maybe not of anyone else's. There was nothing even remotely exotic on her list right now, and her interest was piqued.

"Of course, we don't even know if that *is* blood on it," Mac noted. "Or human, if it is. Could be as stupid as somebody keeping cats out of their garden." He didn't sound convinced.

"I wonder about it being dropped off here," said Andy Patel. "The patrol guys couldn't find anybody on the block who saw it."

"No," said Jenn. "They didn't. The homeowners put the trash out at, ah, eight-thirty in the morning, they said. And then went off to work. So whoever left it had virtually a whole day to do it."

"But in the daylight?" said Mac. "And nobody saw it?"

"Nobody admits they did. But the whole block empties out during the work day, it sounds like. Everybody commutes to something. "

9

Mac thought about his own neighborhood. *He* was home all day, along with a pair of alert and inquisitive dogs. Would he notice someone leaving something by the curb? Only if it happened within two or three houses—the Shepherds would show interest—or if he happened to glance out the window. If he was in the back, if the dogs were out in the back yard, or both, no, he might not have noticed anything at all.

Another point to consider, Mac thought: in Ann Arbor, you can't just put any old thing out with the trash and expect it to be hauled off to the land fill. Each residence, in theory at least, had separate containers for junk, recycling, and compost. With a few exceptions, anything you wanted to dispose of had to go into one of those. So either the donor was just trying to get rid of it quickly, in a panic, or he didn't know much about local garbage service.

"Now, why did I say 'he' there?" Mac asked himself. Somehow, this seemed to him a characteristically male thing to do: making a framework, mounting at least one gun inside it, covering it precisely with canvas, arranging for the gun to go off—maybe even swivel around and go off four times—and then dumping the whole affair on somebody's easement. Would a woman do that? As examples, he considered the women who were standing around; would his wife, Colleen, make something like this? Not in character. Early in their relationship, she'd built a platform bed out of one-by-twelves, using a hammer and nails. That was the most mechanical engineering he could remember her doing, in the course of a thirty-year marriage. Carol, Don's wife? No. She might have some of the skills, but she was a remarkably non-violent person. Jenn Langton? Again, no. Certainly, there must be women somewhere who'd do something like this, but Mac had never met one.

Patel, quite unusually for an FBI agent, was feeling like a fifth wheel. His dinner with Jenn had ended in an unexpected way, and unlike Jenn, he was part of a big, very formal law enforcement organization. He couldn't just volunteer to be put on a case, even if there was any reason why his agency ought to be involved at all. And he still had to get home to his condo in the suburbs. He made his excuses, discreetly ensured that somebody would get Jenn back to her place on the northwest side of Ann

Arbor, and headed out. There was an hour or so left of Saturday, June seventh, 2013.

Southeastern Michigan is largely a coastal plain. Lake Erie, the Detroit River, Lake Saint Clair, and Lake Huron define its eastern edge and its borders with Canada. It's a flat part of the world; you have to go substantially inland before you encounter much in the way of ground relief. In a straight line from a point on the Detroit riverfront, it's a little less than sixty miles west-southwest to the Irish Hills. A little nearer, say fifty miles almost due west, the Sharon Short Hills provide a few feet of altitude. Any closer in, though, and the interesting terrain, what of it there is, is mostly due to river valleys.

In Ann Arbor, a mere thirty-five miles out from the nexus of Detroit, the town rises and falls among a set of contour changes that were created primarily by the Huron River. The Huron divides Ann Arbor unevenly from the northwest to the southeast in about a sixty-forty split, with the smaller portion being north of the river. Mac and Jenn both lived on the southern side, and Jenn's office was there, too. But at eleven o'clock on Monday morning, they were on the north side, specifically *in* he Northside, more properly The Northside Grill, having an early lunch and preparing to go see the device, stripped of its canvas covering and with its secrets, some of them, anyway, exposed.

The Northside wasn't the only home-style or diner-style place in Ann Arbor, nor was it necessarily the first one that would come to mind. Souvenir T-shirts and art prints and so on tended to feature the Fleetwood, a genuine shotgun diner sitting on a goldmine of downtown real estate at Liberty and Ashley. But from a culinary standpoint, the Fleet was just a diner; the food was nothing you hadn't eaten a hundred times before, at a hundred other places. At the Northside, the menu walked a fine line between traditional and unique, and the ingredients, the cooking, and the service were all top notch. Its location put it a short walk from the massive University Hospital complex and right on the edge of a set of neighborhoods extending north and east along Pontiac Trail and Plymouth Road. The customers were doctors, faculty, technical people, IT people, grad students, medical students, and assorted locals. Inside, it was comfortable and unpretentious, decorated in a mix of north woods pine paneling, local art, and ironic found objects. As a sociological measure, the clientele and staff of the Northside exhibited a relatively low ratio of visible tattoos and piercings to overall body surface area.

The two old colleagues were meeting for lunch partly because Jenn wanted Mac's involvement with the device, and she wanted the benefit of his long-practiced ability to separate what was honestly *known* about a case from what a busy and harassed detective might *think* about it. They also needed to meet because Mac was intensely curious about the device, especially since it involved his friends and his neighborhood; he could no longer just waltz into AAPD headquarters by himself and start poking around the evidence room. Actually, he probably could have—everybody knew him—but it saved so much awkwardness if he just went with Jenn. Everybody understood that dynamic: he'd been Jenn's mentor and to some extent, he still was. As long as she didn't mind the appearance of him looking over her shoulder, he didn't mind having her as a chaperone.

They sat down in the east corner booth and ordered. Mac had to think about it and consult his digestive system. He came here often enough that he had favorites, sometimes a big sloppy breakfast sandwich, sometimes a burger. What he ordered depended on how hungry he was, and how hungry typically depended on how his rebellious body was reacting to various treatments and medications. Today, he felt relatively good, and he asked for two eggs scrambled, bacon, and toast. The giant toast slices alone would be more than he ate on bad days. Jenn ordered a salad of some kind.

"So, do we know anything?" Mac started.

"I got some answers from Carter on Sunday," Jenn said, "but I was working a burglary over on Packard, so I didn't have time to go see him." Carter Connelly was what passed for a forensics team at the AAPD; he was not an energy-drink-swilling Goth person like the Pauley Perrette character on TV, nor did he have much in the way of high technology at his disposal. But as a fellow cranky old guy, MacArthur felt good about Carter having the device in his hands. It seemed to be an old guy object, somehow.

"On Packard?" Mac asked. That description was very non-specific, and it could include places very close to Mac's house.

"Not out your way," Jenn said. "Down in student-land. The street past Hoover. Somebody stole a laptop and some money."

"They should just paint 'B and E Target' on those places."

"It's mostly E, not so much B. The kids just won't learn to lock their doors."

What Jenn meant, of course, was that some trusting, drunken, or simply dim student renter had once again left a door unlocked. Someone passing by had looked in, seen something desirable, and made off with it. It happened with such regularity that it was mildly surprising a detective had even had to go on-site. Jenn explained that this time, there was a bit more to it. A neighbor had seen someone, possibly the suspect, running down Arch Street, a block away. And in the dark, the scene lit only by streetlights, the witness wasn't sure, but she thought he might not have been wearing any pants. The witness, Jenn said in a tone of voice intended to mock report language, admitted to having consumed alcohol and appeared uncertain as to whether she was shocked or intrigued by the incident.

"But what Carter said was the thing was a real piece of work," she went on, returning to the device. "He said it looked to him as though it was all handmade or at least hand fitted. Cast iron and brass."

"What *is* it, though? Did he call it a booby trap or what?"

"He didn't say. I was trying to do three things at once, and I didn't get some of his points. He did claim he'd never seen anything like it, and I think he said it had a squash plate."

"A what?"

"He said it was something like a helicopter part."

"A *swash*plate," said Mac. "Yeah, it's a part that controls the rotor blades. I'm having a really hard time seeing ... wait!"

13

"What?"

"He wasn't implying that this thing could *fly*, was he?"

"No, not that he told me. He just said it had this plate."

"We need to see it. I'm not getting this at all."

At the Northside, the entrance is a closet-sized airlock, with a pair of doors, one opening onto the street and one into the restaurant. As Mac and Jenn talked, the inner door opened, and a young man came in. A waitress, flying past with coffee refills, pointed him to an open table at the opposite end of the room. He was tall and very dark skinned, clean-shaven, and his black, wiry hair was cut short. To look at him, you might have thought he was nationally African, not African-American. His face was broad, and his smile at the waitress was a crescent of white teeth. He glanced around as though to see if he knew anyone, then went to his table.

Ann Arbor is not a formal place under most circumstances. Most people dress for comfort, for the climate, or for the hell of it, not to adhere to any current standard of fashion. Mac was in the first category, and the newcomer was probably in the third, since he seemed to have dressed with a certain backward-looking aesthetic. He had on a dark jacket, three-buttoned and slightly longer than a blazer, and under it a plain white shirt. The shirt cuffs stuck out from those of the coat, and they seemed to be gathered at the wrist, without buttons or cufflinks. He was wearing blue jeans over what were probably calf-length black leather boots, and as he sat down, he took off a light-colored linen snap brim cap. At first glance, he didn't look especially unusual. On a second viewing, as the details emerged, he seemed to be a handsome African youth, somehow cast as a clerk in a Dickens novel.

The young man didn't notice Mac and Jenn at all. MacArthur's back was turned toward the door, and he didn't see him enter. Jenn was concentrating on finishing her lunch. She glanced up as he came in and categorized him as a student of some kind. He was. His name was Belonwu, and he was a senior in mechanical engineering at the University. He was born in a Detroit suburb, just as his father and mother had been;

his grandfather was a first-generation immigrant from Nigeria, an Igbo man named Echezonachukwu 'Jerry' Mbanugo.

The detectives paid their tabs and left. They both had vehicles, Jenn's detective car and Mac's pickup truck. The trip downtown was short, just a matter of going west over the Broadway bridge, crossing both the river and the Norfolk Southern railroad. They turned south on 5th Avenue, and Mac grabbed a handicapped space on Ann Street. Jenn parked with the other city vehicles, and waited at the Justice Center's staff entrance as Mac hobbled up slowly. A sunny day helped with the joint pain, but there was just simply a maximum speed he could make on foot, and there was no point in trying to go beyond that. Downstairs, they found Carter Connelly in his tiny work room—no one, including Connelly, would call it a laboratory—with the device using up most of his table space.

"So what kind of crazy stuff are you bringing in here, MacArthur?" he wanted to know.

"Me? Talk to Jenn about that. I'm just along for the ride."

"Well, whatever. This is a real weirdy," Connelly said. "Look at the damn thing."

With its cover off, the device was, as he said, a weirdy. It was a framework of four upright pieces and eight horizontal connections, four at the top and four at the bottom. Each piece was iron of some kind, with ornate touches; there were curves and bends and almost floral whorls, none of which contributed anything structurally. Both of Mac's grandmothers had owned foot-treadle sewing machines, and the device reminded him of those old Singers from the roaring twenties (meaning the sewing machines, not the grandmothers.) In the middle, occupying the cubic space that the outer parts defined, were diagonal arches, also apparently iron, but looking a little more as if they'd been made for the purpose; they were plainer, without ornament. And then, supported by those diagonals, was the weirdest bit of all: a complex arrangement of brass rods and disks and crank arms, connected to four large revolvers.

"Son of a ..." said Mac. "He put four guns into it?" There was that *he* again, as if they already knew the creator of the device.

"Good Lord," was Jenn's comment.

"Yup," said Connelly. "And it's stranger than just that. He put four Italian reproduction black powder guns into it."

"They're what?" said Jenn.

"Modern copies of antique guns. Originals would have been 1860s, 1870s. These were made probably forty years ago. In Italy."

"This is getting kind of creepy," said Mac. "They're cap and ball, black powder pieces, right?"

"That's what I said. You load each chamber with powder and a ball, separately, and then there's a lever under the barrel to mash it all down. No cartridges. Then you put a cap on this ... bump ... back here ..."

Mac kept a straight face. He knew what the 'bump' was actually called, and he was mildly amused at Connelly's reluctance to say 'nipple' in the presence of a lady. He glanced at Jenn; she didn't react.

"Were they all loaded, all twenty-four chambers?" asked Jenn. "They're all six-shooters, right?"

"He just loaded up one chamber each. And all four of 'em were fired."

"Are they all the same model?"

"Well, three of 'em are. The fourth one is the same caliber, but it's got a shorter barrel. All the same manufacturer. All thirty-six caliber. Did I already say that?"

"Explain about the plate," said Jenn. "You said it had a plate ... Mac, what did you call it?"

"Jenn said that *you* said it had a swashplate, Cart, like a helicopter."

"Well, kind of like it, anyway. Look down here at the bottom."

At a point about eight inches from the table surface where the device was resting, there was a disk, articulated in an odd way with a ball joint attached to a vertical rod. Above the disk, bent brass rods attached to it and extended up toward the revolvers. And directly below, there was what seemed to be a weight, linked to the plate by a solid extension, four inches long. Mac shook his head.

"I don't get it, still. What's going on with all that?"

"Is that the trigger?" Jenn suggested.

"Right. Exactly right," said Connelly. "What happens, see, is that weight's a pendulum. And when the pendulum's hanging straight down and not moving, the plate doesn't move. But when it moves right, the plate tips left, and that rod there gets yanked on ... and it fires that gun." He indicated the revolver pointing out one side of the framework.

"But then what? Just one fires?"

"Here's what I thought," said Connelly. "You find this thing, right? And it's in the way or you're curious, and you move it. How would you pick it up?"

"Ah," said Mac. "You'd bend over and put your arms around it ..."

"Yeah. And you stand up, tip it toward you. And the gun on your side, the one pointed right at your chest, well, it goes off."

"And it hits you right in the center of your body," said Jenn. "Center of mass."

"And then, you drop it. Even if it missed you, you drop it. And the pendulum goes crazy and fires the other three guns, too."

"But what a hell of a lot of trouble to go to," Mac said. "I thought these days if you want to make something happen, you just bake a cheap cell phone into it. Cell phones know when they're being tilted, right?"

Connelly shrugged.

"Another thing. How would you set this up without getting shot yourself? I mean, once the guns are loaded and cocked. No safeties, right?"

"They had that figured out," said Connelly. "Down here below the plate, there's a hole. Stick a rod or something through there and everything's locked in place. So you set the whole thing down, pull the rod out, and then it's armed."

"Could you disarm it again if you had to?"

"I guess you could. Lie on the floor, maybe, and poke the safety rod back in. Risky. But if you're lying down, the shots go over you. Maybe."

Jenn was looking the device over closely. "What I don't like about it all, so far, is this: you could pretty much count on it shooting one person, the one who moves it or picks it up. But the other three shots would just be random."

"I don't know if logic is really going to apply, here," said Mac. "I think whoever made this is nuts. Certifiably."

"Maybe. But it works if you know the victim will be alone."

... nor peace, nor help for pain ...

Echezonachukwu 'Jerry' Mbanugo was no longer homesick. He wished earnestly that he was back in London or anywhere else, in fact. The Nigeria in which he was living was not the one he'd longed for. He had returned to Port Harcourt and found that, just as he'd heard, an education was not a guarantee of anything. The job he'd been offered was real enough, but it paid poorly in comparison with his expectations, and he was learning nothing new at all. Three or four days a week, he went into an office and shuffled paper related to rice warehousing. Other days, he would get a phone call from someone he never saw in person. He'd be asked to go somewhere on Wharf Road and count ships. Or take his motorbike to Degema and note what kind of traffic was coming across the river from Edi Kalama. Weekends, he spent at home with his parents, balancing his western experience with their traditionalist approach to life.

18

This went on without any apparent change in tempo, even as the country was sliding toward civil war.

The coup in 1966 changed all that. Igbo politicians and soldiers seized power, prompting a violent reaction by Hausa and Fulani. Refugees from the north and west flooded into the eastern cities. The pressure built and built until in May the next year, the east broke away, declaring itself a separate republic: Biafra.

Jerry got one of his special phone calls a week after that. He was being transferred, the caller said. A hundred and twenty miles northwest to Enugu. That was the capital city of the new Biafra, and the company's office there needed additional staff. He would get a ride with another employee, apparently already making drives back and forth. It was a shock; so far Jerry had been to London and once across the channel to France, just to say he'd been there. Other than that, he'd never been away from Port Harcourt and his family. He obeyed orders, though, since he had no real choice in the matter. The job he had was clearly the only one he was going to get soon, unless he wanted to enlist in the Biafran army. So he went to Enugu.

For the next few months, things ran much as they had. The rice paperwork was almost non-existent now; Jerry spent most of his time gathering information, counting soldiers and trucks and stocks of supplies instead of ships and traffic. Enugu filled up with Igbos from other parts of the country, and some of the non-Igbos left. Race and religion were in the air, like smoke, something you could almost breathe in.

The Biafrans were woefully unprepared to fight a war. Almost all the arms, of all kinds, were in the hands of the government, and the rebel forces were pushed back in a perimeter around Enugu. By October, the town was being shelled, and it was clear that it would fall within days. It was then that Jerry and two of his colleagues got their new orders. The company was going to close its office and move south to Umuahia, following the Biafran leadership. But Jerry and the other two would stay, abandon their office clothes, and pose as locals or refugees. They could take their pick of any role, in fact, that was inconspicuous. They were to do nothing, say nothing, just keep their eyes open. The company would be back in touch with them as soon as it could. If the move to Enugu had been a shock, this was even more so, but again, what else was to be done? They were left with some money and instructions to check once a week, by themselves, never all three together, at one of two addresses in the city. Knock, they were told, and if no one answers, just go away and come back again in a week.

After that, it all fell apart. The rebel government left, the rebel troops left, and the Nigerian army took over. Jerry hid for a week, staying inside, doing nothing at all. When the house he was staying in was commandeered for the occupying forces, he went quietly, without complaining, playing the part of a man from the country with no education or employment. He found a place to set up a lean-to, made of debris from the bombardment, and he gathered containers. Bottles and cans were saleable items, anything that would hold water or gasoline was potentially useful, and he would sit on the side of Abakaliki Road and sell his inventory. This was also the road to the airbase, and when he could keep his mind on it, he noted the military traffic that went by.

From week to week, he walked into the center of the city and knocked on one of the two anonymous doors. For the first months, no one answered. Then, once or twice, he got a response, a small amount of money, and occasionally a request for information. Usually, though, nothing happened. He ate what refugees ate, wore traditional clothing, slept in his lean-to, and heard nothing from his family. In this way, eighteen months went by. Except for the occasional stipends, Jerry lived by scavenging bottles and cans and, for a few trusted Igbo acquaintances, reading and writing letters. He practiced his role; in the same way, another man in the same city, living not far from Jerry's lean-to, was practicing his own profession.

I hate helicopters, Hassan thought. "*I, Hassan bin Sabbagh, the dauntless pilot, the Saracen knight of the air, I am afraid of flying in this damned thing.*" He tried to mock himself into acceptance if not calm acceptance, but it wasn't much use. He truly hated putting his life in the hands of someone else, someone flying an aircraft that was kept in the air by nothing but a giant fan. "*And we're hanging from the fan by one nut, too,*" he thought, trying to keep himself from visualizing the hardware somewhere above his head, the works that kept the rotor attached to the

20

aircraft, gear that a westerner would call the Jesus pin. As a Muslim, Hassan did not call it that; for him, it was just the rotor retaining nut. Even so he prayed earnestly for the well-being of the nut that was currently holding him two hundred or so feet above the ground. In the planes Hassan was used to flying, you either died instantly, blown to atoms in a moment, or you had time to eject. More importantly, in a MiG-17 you could fight back. In this flying delivery van, this Sikorsky Chickasaw, there was no chance for anybody to do anything; there would be nothing at all except a few seconds of horror, preceding a horrific impact.

Hassan was an Egyptian and an officer in the Air Force of the United Arab Republic. He was on detached duty to fly one of a handful of the Mikoyan-built fighters supplied to the Nigerian government for its fight with Biafra. After the Suez fiasco in 1956, after Gamal Abdel Nasser shuffled his aircraft away to the Sudan and to Saudi to escape the British and French invasion, the air arm was not the most admired branch of the Egyptian military. The *Regiment de Parachutistes Coloniaux*, Israeli Mystère fighters, and the British Navy were able to operate against Egypt without concern for air attack. Even in the Sinai, where Nasser's Russian and British-made jets were briefly launched against the Israeli army, they lost heavily and the survivors were quickly pulled back out of harm's way. Once the US and the UN were able to impose a ceasefire (preventing random international aggression was, after all, one of the things the UN was intended to accomplish), the Egyptian Air Force needed a morale boost and an improvement in its public image, and so throughout the early Cold War, it was assigned to make small but visible appearances in the African conflicts of the post-colonial world.

In the Nigerian war, the received idea was that the rebels had no air power at all, little in the way of anti-aircraft defenses, and nothing but camouflage to shield them from air attack. Except for the primitive flight facilities and the transport infrastructure—such as this helicopter, Hassan thought—he didn't consider Nigeria a dangerous posting. He was probably in more peril from his colleagues in the Nigerian military than from the enemy. Although (and here his hand reflexively touched a buttoned breast pocket) as long as he was carrying what he was carrying, almost anyone could be dangerous.

The Marange diamond fields in what was then Rhodesia were just beginning to be known outside Africa. Their production was small, unstructured, and only rudely administered. Uncut gems could find their way into someone's pocket or desk drawer much more easily than in South Africa. From Rhodesia, It was a long, long way to Nigeria, and the traffic in under-the-counter stones was tiny, but it was also highly remunerative. Since no one at the time expected diamonds to be coming out of *West* Africa, the effort to bring them up from the south was worth it; the last jump, north to Europe or across the Atlantic to the US, would be easy and safe. To make it work, you needed reliable people who could move around without interference from inquisitive and greedy officials. If the couriers wore impressive uniforms, so much the better. As a military officer and a citizen of a large and powerful and also African country, Hassan was highly qualified. That he was a Muslim acting in the service of the Muslim-dominated Nigerian government added a great deal to his usefulness. Within a month of arriving in Nigeria, he'd been recruited to move diamonds from a contact in Libreville on the Gabon coast, bring them back to his assigned post outside the city of Enugu, and then discreetly hand them off to a gentleman from Côte d'Ivoire. At that point Hassan would be paid in cash, usually in pounds sterling. His Air Force salary from Nasser's UAR was not princely, and the money he made from this little import/export venture was most welcome.

For those whose images of aviation come mostly from the Vietnam war or later, 'helicopter' probably brings to mind the UH-1—the 'Huey' of *Apocalypse Now* and dozens of other films, not to mention the nightly news. But if you reach a bit farther back, the Sikorsky helos of the Fifties and early Sixties are still iconic. They're big and boxy, and for the technology available, quite successful. They weren't turbine-powered aircraft like later designs; Sikorsky's H-19s and H-34s had huge radial piston engines, a design going all the way back to fixed wing planes of the First World War. This giant pancake sat at an angle, below and in front of the cockpit, and its drive shaft ran diagonally up through the fuselage to the rotor mechanism.

In the specific Chickasaw that Hassan was riding, the engine was running smoothly and noisily, bringing the craft in from the southwest, dropping down the face of the escarpment and across the Ekulu River toward the airbase. It was May, 1969. A year and a half before, the city had been the capital of Biafra, but it had fallen to government forces, and now Hassan and his MiG-17 were based there, flying ground attack missions and harassing planes that were trying to bring in aid to the rebels. As the helicopter lost altitude, Hassan sat up and looked out the yellowed side window; the airbase was bathed in midday sun, and his MiG, along with one of Nigeria's precious few Ilyushin bombers, was parked on the airfield's apron.

The helicopter turned to approach its landing pad near the east end of the runway. The change in aspect brought the control tower into Hassan's view just as a substantial explosion knocked the upper floor right off the tower. The H-19 pilot reacted, jerking the controls, spinning the craft around and away from the smoke and fire. Hassan was on his feet, peering obliquely back through the Plexiglas, trying to see what had happened. The other two passengers, both Nigerian infantry officers, were scrambling for their gear, grabbing for the assorted small arms they carried, panicking, to put it bluntly. Hassan himself had no helmet, just a uniform cap, and nothing more lethal than a *Pistolet Makarova*, a little Soviet officer's sidearm. There was another explosion, this time on the runway.

Suddenly, the H-19 tilted wildly, and one of the Nigerians shouted something incomprehensible. A green shape appeared in the window, headed directly for them. Somehow it managed a climbing turn and missed overhead by a terrifyingly small margin. As it buzzed past, Hassan could just identify it as a plane, a tiny single-engine plane, with—*in the name of Allah!*—rocket pods hanging from the wings.

The plane was a Swedish-built trainer, a two-seat, propeller-driven lightweight produced by Malmö Flygindustri. Five of them had been obtained and brought into Biafra by an international pilot, adventurer, and occasional mercenary, Carl Gustaf von Rosen. Their original white and red coloring was painted over by hand in green and brown camouflage, and each of them carried a pair of rocket launching pods, pods loaded with missiles capable of destroying tanks. The received wisdom about the rebels having no air power was no longer accurate. Today, four of these five 'Biafran Babies' were in the air over Enugu, paying their first visit to the airbase. Their targets were the control tower, any parked warplanes, and anything else that looked military. Von Rosen, two more Swedes, and a Biafran pilot, Augustus Opke, were flying the little craft. The explosions Hassan had seen were von Rosen's first rocket, hitting below the floor of the control tower and his second, near-missing the parked bomber. The next plane, the one that nearly ran into the helicopter, was flown by Opke.

The story about that raid that was still being told by aviation people some forty years on was that at least one of the attackers, allegedly Augustus Opke, hadn't had quite enough training in air-to-ground marksmanship. He expended several of his rockets as he came in low, aiming for Hassan's MiG-17 and missing. Frustrated, he is said to have circled back, landed on the runway, taxied up to pointblank range, and fired a 68mm armor-piercing rocket straight into the side of the parked fighter. Satisfied with the resulting destruction, he then taxied back to the runway and took off again.

Whether or not it really happened that way, *someone* hit the MiG, and it crumpled in a ball of burning jet fuel and black smoke. The helicopter had been angling toward it, the pilot planning on getting away from the chaos and setting down in an open area south of the base. But the smoke and flames from the burning fighter rushed up in front of him, blinding him and—who knows?—perhaps making him think there was a ground attack as well. It may just have been instinctual, flinching away from the horror in front, but he spun the H-19 to the right and at the same time pulled the nose up. The tail dropped, of course, and it bashed into the roof of a hangar, ripping the tail rotor off the aircraft. A helicopter without a tail rotor has nothing to keep the main rotor's torque from spinning the whole aircraft into uncontrollability, and the Chickasaw dropped onto the far edge of the building, tipping over on one side and chopping its main blades to shards as it fell the remaining twenty feet onto the ground, still spinning wildly.

On one of the last revolutions before it hit the ground, Hassan and another of the passengers were thrown against the door. Their combined mass, driven by centrifugal force, was enough to pop the door off its sliding tracks, and both men went out. The Nigerian officer was hurled against the side of the hangar and survived with broken bones. Hassan was less fortunate; somewhere in the air his body intersected with a piece of the disintegrating rotor blades, sharp-edged and moving at high velocity. It killed him as a lance or a spear might have, plunging through his chest and out his back. He may have lived for a few seconds, lying on the ground, or he may have been dead by the time he came to rest. It didn't matter; his fears had been well-founded.

... confused alarms ...

Wednesday morning, June twelfth, was the deadline Emily Weiden had set for herself. Last night had been absolutely as long as she could wait and keep on rationalizing. "*If he still isn't back by tomorrow,*" she'd decided, "*I will have to go out to his house and see if he's there*". And on Wednesday morning, he was not back. His shared office in Haven Hall was exactly as it had been at seven the night before: untouched, a coffee cup with a layer of dried brown on the bottom, two days at least of paper mail in a pile.

Emily was German, born in Düsseldorf, newly arrived in Ann Arbor to do doctoral work in the history of right-wing movements. She was new, new to America, new to the city, not quite as fluent in English as she thought she was. The sheer mechanics of getting a research topic approved, doing the work, writing and defending a thesis in a department that spoke in terms of "Clusters of Interest" instead of topics—these were terrifying to her. She wasn't comfortable with ambiguity. And now, the faculty member she'd been relying on seemed to have vanished. Assistant Professor Allan Kirk had agreed to meet with her on Friday; he hadn't been there, nor had he called. Emily fretted quietly through the weekend, and then watched Monday and Tuesday pass with no change in the situation. By Tuesday afternoon, she gathered the courage to ask one of the Administrative Assistants if Kirk had been heard from. She got little help from the Admin.

At least she knew where Kirk lived. The month she arrived, it had fallen to his lot to host a welcoming party for new students. This used to be left up to the older, tenured faculty with, to put it bluntly, nice houses. Lately, though, a spirit of egalitarianism or simple boredom with the whole thing

25

had led to a top-down policy of sharing the social obligations. Since Kirk was single and as relatively impoverished as young academics typically were, it had been an awkward evening. The students who knew each other gathered together; the faculty clustered too, breaking away periodically to mingle for a few minutes with the new people. Those no one knew, people like Emily, stood by themselves or with another lone person, severely limiting themselves to one glass of box wine and wondering how long it would be before they knew the lay of the land, before they knew that the striking young blonde woman who arrived with the elderly Professor Emeritus was in fact his daughter, not something else? How long before they'd understand why one group would be laughing archly together, then subside into low and respectful tones the next minute as they were joined by a woman whose husband had just died? How long would they have to feel like five-year-olds at a gathering of adults? Emily had not enjoyed herself, but at least she'd saved the photocopied invitation with its sketch map and directions.

She had a car, the money for which had been a gift from her parents. It was a four-year-old Passat, metallic silver, and with a slight odor, still, of its prior owner's cigarettes. She backed it out of its space behind the house of which her apartment was a portion and drove north on State, through one of Ann Arbor's three or four downtowns, the State and Liberty area. Past St. Thomas, State pitched sharply downhill toward the river and simultaneously turned to brick pavement. It ended at Fuller, and she turned right. This was not actually the best way to get where she was going, but it was the route from central campus that Kirk had provided for the new folks. His directions brought her, eventually, to Huron Parkway, then north to Glazier and over to Green Road. She went north to the first opportunity and turned right into a subdivision of approximately middle age. Bounded by Green, Glazier, Earhart, and M-23, it was occupied by a mixed set of lower-level faculty, commuters who liked the easy access to freeways, some retirees, and random others. It looked a bit better now than it had a few years before, when a giant pharmaceutical company had abruptly abandoned north Ann Arbor, but there were still houses for sale.

In fact, the north end's financial troubles were the reason Professor Kirk lived there. He was renting a house whose owners had been forced to move east, following the husband's job; it was a small, single-story home.

Thanks to the landscaping, the primary thing you could see from the front was the garage; trees and shrubs were slowly obscuring the rest of the house. The entrance door was tucked back in a recess defined by the garage wall and the front room. Emily parked on the street.

She was uncomfortable. Distinctly so. To her, Kirk was an important person, important because he was the first of a number of older people, people higher up the ladder of academic achievement, who would have to approve of her work and guide it and criticize it over a period of six or seven years. He was the next person in a long list of people she'd have to please and impress before she could even begin to think of moving up herself, of getting to the next level, competing for one of a few available positions around the world, living in rented houses or apartments, concerning herself with conferences and conventions and published works. To his peers, Doctor Kirk was quite a low-ranking member of the community, with his reputation still to be established and the grail of tenure still a long way off. But to Emily, he was a point of contact with her future. Now, she was about to go up to his house, ring his doorbell, and in effect ask, "Why did you not show up for work?" The situation was far outside her comfort zone.

She looked at the house, remembering it as it had looked at night with snow on the ground. *What will I say if he's there?" she asked herself." What if he's angry at being disturbed? Well, I will say I was worried. I will say that I thought perhaps he might have been sick. It doesn't seem anyone else has checked on him, though. No one else is worried. Does that make me seem odd?*

She saw that there was a car in the drive, parked close to the garage door. That seemed like a good sign; she had no idea what Kirk drove, but a car of any kind suggested that someone was in the house. She knew from the party that he was not married, not in a living-together relationship with anyone, at least that he was admitting. What would she say if someone else answered the door? And of course, what would she do if no one did?

Emily made up her mind and got out of her car. She went up the driveway, past what turned out to be a small Honda, and paused at the door to listen. Nothing. She pressed the doorbell. She could hear it chime. Nothing happened. She waited a measured sixty seconds and rang again.

Another minute passed, and no one came to the door. Her stomach began to hurt; now, she'd reached the limits of her planning. She hadn't decided what she'd do if the result of coming up here and bothering a faculty member at home turned up ... nothing. Would she go back to the department and face the cranky Admin again, could she say, "I'm worried about Doctor Kirk," or "I went to his house and nobody was there"? At the back of her mind was the thought that this was somehow a misdeed, a breaking of some unwritten rule: *You never call on faculty at home without an invitation!*

To the left was a picture window, without blinds or curtains. Without approaching it, she allowed herself to turn in that direction and look in. The front room it showed her was more or less as she remembered it, with a couch and a chair, not much in the way of decoration. A floor lamp was on, strangely enough at this time of day. No one was visible.

Playwright Lane was a quiet street, at least in the middle of the day. Children would be in their last week or so of school, adults would be at work, mostly. But now Emily heard a small gas engine start up, close by. She turned and saw that across the street, an older woman wearing ear protection had just started her lawn mower. Emily rang the doorbell once more; this time the chime was drowned by the mower. She made a decision.

She walked back down the driveway and across the street. The woman with the ear muffs was working away from her, and Emily waited on the sidewalk until the neighbor turned and started back. Emily waved her hand slightly. The woman reached down and turned off the mower; she pulled the muff away from her right ear.

"Can I help you?" she asked.

"Yes, good day," said Emily. "I am a student of the professor who lives over there. Do you know if he is at home?"

"Why, no, I don't. Did you ring? That's his car, I think."

"Yes, I did ring, but no one answers. He has not been to the department, the school in," Emily paused, "three days now."

"Well, I don't know. I don't really know him. He's only been here a year or so."

"Thank you. If you do see him ... would you say for me that we are concerned about him?" The *we* was of course, a falsehood. As far as Emily knew, nobody else was concerned at all. Defeated, she turned and walked back to her own car. The neighbor watched her go. She was still watching as Emily drove away, then circled back, for no good reason at all, and drove slowly by again. Nothing had changed, and Emily gave up.

From being puzzled, Mrs. Amanda Cole, the woman with the lawn mower, had suddenly become concerned herself, not about Kirk and his whereabouts but about this young woman with an accent who was driving around her neighborhood. Property crime was really the only thing most Ann Arbor residents were aware of, and the police frequently encouraged the population to report 'suspicious' behavior. To Mrs. Cole, Emily seemed to qualify, and she went inside to her phone.

A few minutes after that, an Ann Arbor patrol officer cleared from a theft report call at Huron High, a mile and a half away. She was asked to check on suspicious activity on Playwright Lane, with a description of an actor and car but no license plate recorded. It hadn't occurred to Mrs. Cole to note Emily's plate. When the officer got there, Mrs. Cole recounted the conversation she'd had with the young lady, and although the officer, Jeri Klein, privately discounted Emily as being suspicious, she was interested in the non-appearing faculty member. It was worth a look, she decided, just to see if the house had been broken into.

Klein walked across the street and essentially repeated what Emily had done, glancing at the car, ringing the bell, looking in the window. But being a cop and in uniform, she had no reservations about going further. She tried the front door, finding it locked. Likewise, the garage door was secured. Then she walked around to the right side of the house, where the blank south wall of the garage and a property-line honeysuckle hedge left about two feet of pathway. She came out into the back yard and a green twilight, even at half-past twelve, since the place was dominated by three large deciduous trees, maples or oaks, now in full leaf and effectively filtering and coloring most of the sunlight. The honeysuckle went on around all three sides, making it a very private space. In the back

29

wall of the house, a sliding glass door gave access to a simple deck, probably original and in need of refinishing. But closer to where Klein was standing was a door into the back of the garage, and it was standing open.

"*Well, that's not good*," she thought, and looked in. The garage itself was mostly empty, and the lights were on, two bare bulbs in fixtures screwed into roof joists. There was a set of four cast concrete steps from the floor up to an entrance door. That door was open, and a man was lying half in and half out of it, with his legs trailing down the steps.

... drear and naked shingles of the world ...

It was after dinner. Mac and Colleen were sitting at their kitchen prep island; when it wasn't occupied with prep, it doubled as a kind of in-house bar. There was a bowl or two of snacks and the remains of the evening's bottle of wine. They'd been talking about local news, about yet another southeastern Michigan city government in deep trouble—*deep yogurt*, as an old acquaintance used to say—because of simple and very poorly-concealed corruption.

"I think," Colleen said, "organizations have ages like people."

"What?" said Mac. He'd missed part of what she said and mixed up what he did hear with his own ponderings.

"I said organizations age. They go through stages."

"Explain, explain, explain," said Mac.

"What?"

"Kipling. One of the *Just So Stories*. 'How the First Letter was Written'. The chief of a tribe, hopping on one foot, shouting *Explain, explain, explain!*"

One of the more irritating things about MacArthur was his storeroom of a mind, full of obscure and useless snips of information and literature, accessed by a poorly-designed, undocumented, and unreliable search engine. His tangents weren't just irrelevant, they could be conversation-pathologic, boarding someone else's train of thought like the James gang, waving carbines and screaming "Where's the gold?" After thirty years, Colleen could see this coming and knew how to take evasive action. Like General Roberts marching to Kandahar, you just had to carry on.

"The older you get," she said, "the more you manage risk. If you're smart. A young person skates by for a while with, I don't know, just enough insurance to get his car licensed."

"Okay," said Mac.

"Young people, young organizations. They can't afford to manage risk, or they don't do it very well. They rely on luck. Or they count on being young and healthy enough to recover from whatever goes wrong. But you get older. When you can afford it, if you're paying attention, you start buying down your risks. You buy insurance. You save some of your money. If you're really smart, you diversify."

"Yeah."

"But I think what that does is desensitize you to risk. You think it's dealt with. Problem solved. You've got the reserve fund, the rainy day fund, auditors ... and you start to ignore warning signs. "

"Like what?"

"Like changes in your market. Changes in population. Changes in culture. Your management spends its time fighting each other instead of the competition. Aging employees, aging customers, aging citizens. Relationships with vendors getting too comfortable."

"So you turn inward, is that what you mean?" Mac asked.

"Yes, inward, I guess. That's part of it, anyway. You're not looking at the rest of the environment any more. But you get into routines, too. Trivia. You wake up in the morning and say, '*We still have all these problems, but today I've got six meetings and a lunch date and I have to pick up my prescriptions ...* ' And then you come home and have dinner and go to bed, and next morning, nothing's changed, and the big issues are twenty-four hours worse."

"For a while, still, you get your pay check."

"Right. And your City-owned car and your driver and your Administrative Assistant."

"But there are corrupt and criminal young guys, too," said Mac. "New companies that are rotten from the start. New cities ... look at the cattle towns out west. In the nineteenth century. Or shanty towns anywhere. They're run by gangs from day one."

"Sure. But I'm talking about the normal case, not the outliers. I'm talking about a predictable thing. Like the idea of disease staging. Maybe this ... decline, you could say ... is something preventable. If you catch it early."

"Well," said Mac, "He didn't think of the disease staging analogy, but as a thesis goes, David Halberstam beat you to it, thirty-five, thirty-six years ago."

"You mean *The Reckoning*? The giant book about Nissan? I didn't know you'd read that."

"I didn't know *you* had."

"Part of the MBA ... I think there's a copy downstairs somewhere."

"I know. It looked interesting." Another irritating thing about Mac: he was a natural speed-reader.

"The thing about that book," said Colleen, "is it's not prescriptive. It's a kind of history, but it doesn't present solutions."

"Are there any?" asked Mac. "I mean, would you expect a documenter like Halberstam to dream up a cure for cancer while he was writing about the history of oncology?"

"A cure? No, I don't think so. But I'm talking about symptoms, anyway, not the disease. Maybe two different diseases. One of them, the shantytown/Wild West thing you mentioned: that's more like an infection. It's acute. There's a known cause. People have nothing, and they do what they can to get something and make it to the next day.

What I'm rambling on about is a different underlying condition. Call it corporate cancer, organizational malignant ... things. The inflexibility, inaction, denial, this inward-looking stuff, corruption. Those are symptoms. The cause ... well, sorry to say it, but it's basically age. It's stuff wearing out and not being replaced."

There was a pause. Goose had been napping at the foot of Mac's bar stool, and Snacker had her head under Colleen's. Mac picked out a couple of pretzels and gave one to each dog, Snacker first as protocol required.

"So what happens to a city," Colleen went on, "when all of a sudden, all your middle-aged, risk-managing, diversified population panics and moves out to the suburbs? Or they get laid off and *have* to move. And you're not ready? You have no plan?"

"And you still have a guy whose job is to process traffic tickets ..."

"Yeah," said Colleen, "and someone who issues building permits. But nobody whose job description says 'Plan for existential catastrophe'. And you're screwed."

"*Things Fall Apart.* Yeats *and* Chinua Achebe. I see what you mean."

The city of Gardner, Michigan, was certainly screwed in the sense Colleen meant and in just about any other sense as well. It was one of Detroit's near-in suburbs, settled in the Forties and established as a city in the mid-Sixties. It had never had much in the way of its own industry or even retail, just rows and rows of houses for the people who worked in other cities, at Ford's (as they called it,) and Chrysler and Packard and the thousands of smaller firms that supported the auto business. The war didn't make much social difference; the sons went off to fight, maybe, but the fathers and mothers and daughters got up and went to work in the morning. Building munitions wasn't especially different from building cars, and nuts and bolts were still nuts and bolts, whether they held trucks together or tanks.

After the war, the boom carried on. The GIs came home and wanted a tangible reward for giving up a chunk of their youth. They wanted wives and cars and appliances and a place to live. More and more of those small, undistinguished homes went up, lining streets with unimaginative names: Elm and Maple. Main and Central. Cherry Lane. There were a few bigger houses, but the average place was nine hundred or a thousand square feet, all in one story, plus a basement. The footprint was a simple rectangle, with a roofline pitched in parallel to the street. They were usually built of brick, without ornament, and they were more strictly utilitarian than anything Frank Lloyd Wright ever drew. With electricity, water, and some kind of heat—coal or fuel oil, to begin with—they were a place to live, and for the original occupants, Gardner was often a much, much better place than they'd experienced before. The war brought tens of thousands of poor people to the Detroit factories, coming from crowded East Coast cities, the South, even the Western and plains states. They were Black, Irish, Polish, Italian, German. Many more of them, from families already living in Detroit or in one of its ethnic enclaves, looked for homes outside the big city limits, mostly for reasons of price and availability. A substantial number of them found Gardner.

The town grew and wrangled with its neighbors over boundaries and revenue. Incorporation as a city was just a formalization of its status. It had a name, a city government, and a tax base of sorts, but not much else. People voted and slept and paid taxes in Gardner, but they shopped in other places and worked in other cities, and as long as the water flowed from the faucet and the lights came on, they didn't pay much attention to the civic entity. There was a school system that excelled in its mediocrity; it was neither especially bad nor particularly good. In the year of incorporation, there were neighborhoods and houses and streets that were nearing thirty years old. It was not a new town by any measure, just a new city.

The first governments in Gardner were people who were essentially volunteers, people who ran friendly, bland campaigns for Mayor and City Council, acting not out of a desire to enter politics but in the spirit of preserving a comfortable and unchallenging place to live. Incorporating was a defensive measure, for the most part, designed to keep the surrounding municipalities from annexing the place away a block at a time. The big change for many residents, at first, was that they wrote 'city treasurer' instead of 'township treasurer' on their property tax checks.

Of course, no one in Gardner gave a thought to, for example, the situation in Central Europe and the Balkans during the period before the First World War. Why would they? What comparisons could there be, what lessons could be learned? How could their situation be compared to that of small countries, living in the shadows of Austria-Hungary or Russia? Someone reading *The Proud Tower* or *The Guns of August* might have seen some similarities, though, if they'd stopped to consider. Off to the east of Gardner, only ten miles away, was the giant metropolis, the elephant in the room, Detroit. Detroit's fortunes ruled the fortunes of the near-in suburbs, and when Detroit exploded in racial anger, and the last of its even moderately affluent residents fled to the outer ring of towns, Gardner's middle class population went too. Tax revenues plummeted, officials resigned and left. It wasn't quite as bad as being pulled into an apocalyptic world conflict, but it was bad enough.

Thirty-five years later, Gardner looked worse, in some ways, than Detroit. In the big city, when the Council, the Mayor, and the state could stop bickering with each other long enough, they tore down abandoned houses. In Gardner, things just stayed where they were and declined. In the older neighborhoods, the sidewalks were like paving stones, each rectangle of old concrete separated from the others by grass and weeds growing up through the spaces. Driving those streets, you'd see almost nothing new or current. Big, older cars; a weathered Quonset hut, surrounded by chain link fence; junk yards and scrap metal businesses; in the middle of a block, a pair of store fronts, long closed, with that urban rarity, a pay phone on a pole; on the street itself, one lonely scrawl of graffiti; free-standing basketball hoops, right out in traffic, if there had been any traffic; one woman pushing a stroller, just walking, not walking *to* anywhere, since there would be nowhere to go, no place to buy a loaf of bread, no destinations at all except blocky, yellow-brick church buildings, churches that contributed nothing except to enable cliques and individual frustrations. Everywhere, the same ancient and crumbling pavement.

If you turned wrong, you'd find yourself following a long east-west street, cracked and heaving, and with nothing on the north side but scrub trees and a railroad right of way. Without warning, the street would simply end. The final few lots would be empty with the exception of the last one;

there'd be a house there, slowly leaning backward. The chipboard nailed over the doors and windows would be the newest, brightest thing about it. Around you, on the ground, there would be no cans and bottles, no trash, no condom wrappers, no needles. If you walked away from the street and pushed through the sumac and ailanthus into the open land, you'd be able to see a hundred and fifty yards north to the railway, but you'd see nothing else, no dumped guns, no torched cars, no bodies. Not even the most basic human behaviors—sex, eating, addiction, crime— would bring people to this lonesome edge. Especially on a gray day, you might think you'd come not just to the end of the road, but to the end of the world.

... you hear the grating roar of pebbles ...

Jenn Langton was at her desk, for a change. There were four such desks in one room, each with a detective or another kind of 'inside' cop, that is, someone other than a supervisor or patrol officer, in possession. Jenn used to spend the bulk of her time in the office, at this desk, because she found paperwork and phone calls less threatening than going out into the city and inviting trouble. Lately, she'd been on the streets more of the day. She was coming to accept that investigating things did actually require you to see people, ask them questions, and make them uncomfortable. She still wasn't entirely comfortable with making people uncomfortable, but her level of comfort with it was increasing.

She was forty-X. As much as she'd have liked to forget it, she knew to the day the value of X. It was two, in fact; she was forty-two and not especially resigned to it. Her hair hadn't been much of an issue for her through her thirties, but now she was coloring it, turning its original light brown into something closer to blonde. With her light complexion, it worked fairly well. For her age and the amount of stress her life had involved, she could look conventionally pretty when she took the trouble; and when she occasionally affected a pair of aviator sunglasses, a duty shotgun, and a body-armor vest, she was probably someone's feminine ideal. That was not a person she wanted to meet, however. Her ex-husband had a thing for women cops, and he was now being made unhappy by at least one and possibly two of them. Jenn wished all three of them joy of their decisions.

Louie Burke, younger and even newer as a detective, banged the door open and ran, literally, for his desk. As he struggled to get his sport coat on, he started talking, fast and loudly as was his usual practice.

"Jeez, Jenn, got a homicide, looks like! I'm up! Never had one before! Looks like a shooting! You hear about any missing person stuff? Guy hadn't been seen for a while. Maybe a break-in. Up north, off Green Road. You seen my keys?"

Jenn held up a hand. "Stop," she said, pitching her voice in only a slightly more comradely manner than she used to use on prisoners at the county jail. "You said a shooting?"

"Yeah, that's what it says! Did I leave my car keys on your desk?" Burke ignored her tone and body language, again as usual.

"No, Burke. You hung them back up where they're supposed to be. Over there. Before you go any further off the edge, what's going on? I've got a case with guns and without a victim. I might be interested."

"Oh. Thanks," he said, grabbing the keys to a detective car off a peg board. "Yeah, you got that weird box thing, right? Pistols in it or something?"

"Right. Pistols. So somebody's shot?"

"Yeah! That's all I know. Gotta get up there!"

"Hold on thirty seconds then, and I'll go with you."

There had been a time when she would have been relieved not to have a homicide on her plate. Later on, she might have hesitated to butt in on someone else's case. At least, she would have sought permission first. But lately, she was getting more aggressive. She was less interested in "How do I close this?" than in "Why did it happen?" And anything that might shed some light on that damn device and its squash plate was certainly on her own priority list, if not precisely on her sergeant's. She took her city car and the last she saw of Burke, he was trotting off toward his.

There are people who see the world from a cartographic point of view: north is up, south is down, streets can be assembled into the edges of a network with nodes that represent your location and destinations; getting from point A to point B is a process of identifying alternatives and selecting from among them. Jenn was one of those, Burke was not, so it was no surprise that she got to the address on Playwright Lane ahead of him. There were four patrol cars, some number greater than four patrol officers, and already a web of yellow tape being strung. She parked far enough away to present no obstacles to ambulances, fire trucks, hazmat teams, or whatever else might need to get in close, and walked up the sidewalk. Jeri Klein was directing human traffic, sending official personnel around to the garage back door, sending neighbors away, politely but firmly away. She knew Jenn, of course, and had an immediately conflicting pair of reactions; as a woman officer, she found other female cops easier to work with; as someone with ambitions in the department, Jeri saw Jenn as a bit of a rival figure. At the moment, though, she was mostly just happy to see a detective show up.

"Hello, Detective," she said. "Victim's in the garage. Back door was open. We haven't opened anything else up yet."

"Thanks. It's actually not my case. Louie Burke will be here in a minute."

"Oh. Okay. Right up beside the garage is the way to go, anyway."

"All right. I'll just go take a look. When Burke gets here, he can decide what he wants to do about doors."

Jenn went around the house to the back side and nodded to the patrol officers who were there, ostensibly checking the yard itself, in fact doing as little as they could. Crime scene investigation was what the damn detectives got paid for, after all.

Keeping off the garage floor, Jenn stuck her head in the open door and looked around. The dead man—Burke had said 'a guy', and the shoes the body was wearing tended to support that assessment of gender—was just about half in and half out of the house proper, with his legs down the garage steps. There was an odor of decomposition, enough to indicate that he or something, anyway, had been dead for several days. Jenn noted that from this restricted point of view, it wasn't clear whether the attack (if there had been an attack) had been in the garage and the victim had managed to make it part way into the house, or if he'd been coming in and had been shot, stabbed, bludgeoned, or simply frightened to death by someone already there. To the dead man, it made no difference at all, but it would make quite a difference to the investigation.

Women in non-uniformed police assignments face a different set of challenges than men do when it comes to carrying gear. Jenn had solved her cargo needs by investing in three blazers or sport coats, all from the same line of clothing and all selected for certain features. They were made of heavier cloth than most fashion items, came with two external pockets and one internal, and they could be modified by a clever seamstress to have one more pocket, chest high and inside. They were cut loosely enough to cover a sidearm, worn on the left in a shoulder holster, and Jenn was able to distribute her most critical gear among the pockets. Now, she took out her flashlight from the inside right, and crouched down near the ground. Shining the light laterally, she looked for tracks, marks, stains, anything at all on the garage floor.

Cars, like children, track mud in, and even the most meticulous housekeepers don't necessarily clean up after them frequently. Jenn's own garage floor, she remembered, was still sporting a vast brown stain from a cup of coffee dropped five or six months ago. This garage had a typical coating of dust and dried crud; footprints might show up, stains certainly would; she'd have to remind Burke to get pictures first, before he let people wander around in here.

It wasn't a large garage. It would have taken one big car or a small one and a quantity of stored junk. It was remarkably junk-free, though. Aside from some cardboard boxes stacked along the north wall, it was empty. Jenn pointed her light down at the immediate floor, then along the back wall, left and right. There was nothing there in the way of tools, show shovels, leaf rakes; right at her feet, there were indications that a car had been pulled in all the way, as though it were a full sized sedan or an SUV, not the compact that was sitting out front. Tire marks and a small stain— oil or coolant—suggested that at least one vehicle had needed all the room there was. The little Honda sitting in the driveway wouldn't have had to pull in all the way, but maybe the driver just preferred to.

Out in the middle of the floor, there appeared to be some disturbances in the surface dirt. At least, from this distance, they looked like disturbances. Otherwise, there wasn't a great deal to be seen. The walls were unfinished, bare studs and ceiling joists exposed. Thinking of the device, Jenn ran her eyes along the walls, looking for holes, damage, anything other than two by fours and exterior plywood. Nothing obvious appeared.

"And speaking of nothing appearing," she thought, *"where the hell is Burke?"* She put the flashlight away and walked back around to the front of the house. Jeri Klein was still there; no Burke.

"Have you heard anything from Detective Burke?" Jenn asked.

"Nothing. I was going to come and ask you."

"That's funny. I could call him, I suppose."

As Jenn reached for her phone, it started to ring. It was displaying a number she didn't recognize, and she answered the call with "Detective Langton?" spoken with a tone and inflection that conveyed the question "Are you sure you have the right number?" along with the hope that the call was actually a mistake. It was a habit she was trying to break and replace with something more confident, but she hadn't shaken it off completely.

"Jenn? It's Louie. Listen, I got a problem."

"Burke? What's going on?" In the background, she could hear a certain amount of random noise, overlaid with an arriving siren.

"I got in an accident! Guy ran a stop sign and T-boned me!"

"Are you all right?"

"Yeah, I'm okay. I mean, pretty much. But the other guy is hurt, they're going to transport him. Listen, can you take the homicide up there?"

"Did you call the Sergeant?"

"Yeah, he said he'd call you. Since you were there already, I mean."

"All right, Burke. I can take the case. Are you going to the hospital?"

"No, I'm okay. Really. But you know, all the paperwork. It's a real hassle. I'll be tied up for hours!"

"Actually more like weeks, sonny," Jenn thought. She'd bumped a city car against a wall, once, and the resulting chaos cost more in taxpayer dollars than the repairs did. "Don't worry about it," she said. "I'll call the Sergeant myself if he doesn't call me. I'll talk to you later on."

"Okay, Jenn, thanks a lot." Burke hung up.

Klein was watching closely.

"That was Burke," Jenn said. "He has a ... problem. Looks like I'm working this one."

"Good," said Jeri.

A few hours later, several facts were established and a few other things strongly indicated. Among the facts were the identity of the victim, Assistant Professor Allan Kirk, PhD.; the cause of death, namely a gunshot wound in the upper chest; and the name of the young woman who had been looking for him. The latter information came quite easily; Jenn called the History Department and was instantly pointed at Emily Weiden, since Emily had just a few minutes before mustered enough courage to bother the Admin again. Emily was invited to provide a statement.

Another set of facts: the marks that Jenn thought she saw from the back garage door were actually there, and they seemed to involve footprints, scratches in the dust and even in the concrete floor itself, and several bloodstains in a line from the place where Kirk was lying to a spot roughly in the middle of the garage. Further, there was an impact hole in the cement, not far from the first of the bloodstains, and it appeared to contain the smashed remnant of a lead bullet.

A thing that was less than established fact but certainly seemed likely was the notion that Kirk had somehow been killed by the pistol device. Jenn stood a bit to the side of the spot where he had most likely been shot and looked around the walls. Facing east, toward the back wall, she imagined Kirk picking up the device, tilting it, and being shot in the chest. That would leave three other pistols to fire, one straight ahead and one to each side. The left side gun was probably responsible for the hole in the floor, meaning that the device had tipped over radically in that direction. Therefore, the right side shot should have gone south and up. Sure enough, a few inches short of the ceiling, there was a hole in the plywood. It was matched on the outside by a hole in the plastic siding; from there, the bullet would have carried on, over the house next door, and fallen somewhere, probably harmlessly, on down the block.

The last shot, though, was another matter. There was no evidence of an impact, no damage to the east wall or its window and door, nothing on the floor in that direction, no holes in the roof. All four guns in the device had gone off; Carter Connelly was sure of that. Somehow, one of them had managed not to hit anything or at least not anything Jenn could find.

It had been quite a long day, and it was going to be a longer night, getting things squared away and written down. Jenn was on her way back into the office when a thought struck her. She hadn't called MacArthur.

... the breath of the night-wind ...

Jerry Mbanugo lay flat on the ground behind his lean-to and covered his head with his arms. The explosions had stopped, but small arms fire was everywhere. Nigerian troops were firing into the air, into the bush outside of town, at each other, at nothing. The Hausa/Fulani peoples were warriors by cultural background, but the young men serving with the government in 1969 had inherited nothing of that tradition except spirit. Discipline was not their strong suit.

Jerry had no idea what was going on. Explosions meant mortars, or someone using full-blown artillery, or even air attack, and at least until today the Government had been doing most of that. If they were now shooting at themselves, that would be a good thing from an Igbonationalist point of view, but in the near term, it would make Enugu a very dangerous place for him to be. From where he was lying, he could see almost nothing. To the north, his own hut blocked the view of Abakaliki Road, and the building it was leaning against cut off any sight of the airbase. To the south, away from town, there was nothing to see except brush and rock, and westward to his left there were three vacant lots. Other refugees had set up tents and ad hoc shelters there, but the Army had ousted them in the last few days. They left Jerry alone, probably because his establishment looked slightly more formal and permanent or because his used cans and bottles were occasionally useful. Now, he was thinking frantically of next moves. Whatever was happening, he could have no part to play except to stay alive and at liberty. If he could gather some scraps of information, he might pass them along when he could. In the near term, the questions were simple: stay here? Go somewhere else to hide? Where?

He waited too long. A group of soldiers, four or five of them, in a mix of camouflage and plain green uniforms, appeared on the road, trotting toward the airbase and herding a dozen civilians. One of the armed men broke away and grabbed Jerry by the arm, saying "Get up! Get up! Come along!" He was shoved into the group, and all of them were prodded into an uncoordinated run.

"What do they want?" he managed to gasp at the man beside him.

"To clean up. At the airbase. Save people," the man said between breaths.

It was no more than a quarter-mile's run to the gate of the airbase. The firing was tapering off, but excited and nervous troops were still shooting. As the group jogged past a building, a shot from somewhere broke a second-floor window; some of the civilians swerved, paused, sped up, slowed down, began shouting, and generally showed signs of panic. The soldiers weren't having any, though, and with the butts of their assorted rifles they kept the movement under control and headed in one direction. At the gates—closed and guarded—there were officers and a pair of trucks with pintle-mounted machine guns. The corporal in charge of the group spoke briefly with a captain, and the gates were swung open. The civilians started to go through, but the corporal waved furiously at the trucks.

"No, idiots! Get on the trucks! Do you want to walk everywhere? Move!"

Jerry did not really want to get on a truck nor did he want to be on the airbase, but it was no time to stand out. He helped an older man get up into the truck bed and then jumped up himself.

The truck was an International flat bed, somewhat battered and rusted out. There was a single Browning machine gun mounted on a pintle at the front corner of the bed, just a vertical length of pipe, welded in. Without warning, the truck hit a chuckhole, and as it did so, the machine gun came untied and spun around on its mounting. The barrel whacked an elderly Igbo gentlemen on the side of the head. "Christ!" he said.

One of the two Nigerian soldiers riding with them jumped up as though to attack him or at least remonstrate with him. The other guard pulled his colleague back. "There'll be plenty of time for that later on," he said in Hausa. He pushed the old man aside and re-secured the machine gun with a piece of cord. The truck slowed and stopped in front of a pair of hangars. One of the guards grabbed the older gentleman, pointed to Jerry, and told them both to jump off. "Work here," he said.

"What do we do?" asked Jerry.

"Clean up! Clean up! Put things in bags!" The guard threw a couple of burlap shipping bags in his direction. The truck drove away.

Jerry looked around. Straight ahead was an empty space between two hangars; in the middle of it there was a huge mess that apparently had been a helicopter. He could see at least two, possibly three bodies, and none of them was moving. The helicopter seemed to have crashed down between the two buildings; there was obvious damage to the side of one of the hangars where pieces of the aircraft or the aircraft itself had smashed into it. Two of the bodies were also lying near the base of the hangar wall. They were both wearing uniforms of one kind or another, one a Nigerian green uniform and one in a sandy brown color that Jerry hadn't seen before. The third body was behind the wreck; all he could see was a foot sticking out.

Beyond the wreckage to the south was open scrub land; they were right at the edge of the developed part of the city. Behind them of course was the runway and the rest of the airbase. On either side they were enclosed by the hangar walls. The older man—Jerry had seen him on Abakaliki Road but didn't know his name—seemed to be looking to Jerry for instructions or directions.

"I think we should look busy," said Jerry. He picked up one of the bags and held it out. "You go on the other side of the crash. Fill this with papers or things that belong to the people. Not the junk. Look in the pockets of the body, too." The old man just nodded. He was dazed; the absurdity of using a burlap bag to clean up a helicopter crash didn't seem to strike him. He just took the bag and shuffled off out of sight around the back of the fuselage.

Jerry took the other bag and started toward the bodies lying against the hangar. One of them, a Nigerian Hausa officer, was alive. He was unconscious but still breathing. A startlingly white fragment of bone stuck out of his left hip, and there was a substantial pool of blood on the ground. Jerry moved past him and examined the other body, the man in the brown uniform. He was neither Hausa nor Fulani, but some northern African type that Jerry didn't recognize. The insignia on his uniform were in Arabic. He was not alive.

The situation at the moment was distinctly perilous. Jerry, who was obviously an Igbo, was in the middle of the aftermath of an attack on a government airbase, and that attack would certainly be blamed on Igbos. He was surrounded by Nigerian government troops, and all of them would consider him an enemy militarily, ethnically, religiously, and politically. He was also not what he was pretending to be; although he had nothing in his possession that would suggest he was an educated young man, working for an American company, he certainly was guilty of being and doing those things, and it would not be too much of a stretch to imagine the government troops finding out. He glanced around. No one was watching; the old man was out of sight, uselessly stuffing pieces of broken helicopter into a burlap bag. The truck with its workers and soldiers was gone, further down the airfield where presumably it was attending to the

45

demolished control tower. Jerry's immediate instinct was just to walk south out into the bush and keep on walking. He almost did.

Then he glanced down at the dead man lying at his feet. On the man's left side, threaded on his belt, was a small brown holster, and it obviously contained a pistol. Although the last thing Jerry wanted to be caught with was a pistol, it suggested that the man might have other, more useful things. Looking nervously around, Jerry bent down and began going through the man's uniform. He found a bit of money in one pocket and in another, sealed in a paper envelope, there was something that felt like a dozen or so small, hard objects. He was about to investigate when the old man knocked over a piece of debris and made a noise doing it. The noise reinstated Jerry's paranoia, and he simply stuffed the money and the paper pouch in his pocket and walked as quietly as he could away between the two hangars and out into the scrub trees.

Jerry was not a country-raised man. He'd spent his young life in Port Harcourt and then gone abroad to London. London was much less scary for him than it was for some of his associates and colleagues. One of them was a young man who'd done well in a local school; when he made it to London, he was so terrified by the city that he stayed in his apartment and learned only how to get to his classes and to a few of the low-end eating establishments in the area. He never went anywhere else. Not Jerry. For him, the urban network of London made sense. It was bigger and more intense and there were more different kinds of people, but streets were streets, corners were corners. Even if a street came to an end, it came to an end. It didn't just taper off into sand, rock, and thorn trees. Now Jerry was alone, barefoot, in the middle of completely abandoned, uninhabited African countryside. Here every tree grabbed at your clothing with thorns. Underfoot, who knew? Snakes certainly, scorpions perhaps. When he stopped and turned west he was only a quarter mile from the city or the edge of the city. But he was as unhappy and he felt as vulnerable as if it'd been miles. The average height of the bush was about at his shoulders, and he walked stooped to keep his head out of sight. He'd look up from time to time to make sure he wasn't drifting away further from the comfort of the town.

46

He felt a strange conflict. Enugu itself was a place that harbored little but the possibility of arrest, physical injury, probably death, and yet he longed for it. He understood buildings and streets and alleys, the bush he did not. He feared the things that were in the town, but the town itself beckoned him back. It offered an end to this ceaseless up-and-down, back-and-forth of his head as he watched for thorns, struggled to keep his shirt from catching in them, watched his feet for vipers, and ducked his head up to see if he was off course. This went on for a period of time indeterminate, sometimes moving more slowly than he should have, sometimes faster than was wise. He looked up to check the distance to the town, and froze in a sudden panic. From the corner of his eye he saw movement ahead, heard a noise, twigs snapping. He ducked back down, just in time to see a small animal bolt away, its tail up high. To Jerry the noise it made seemed extremely loud, loud enough to give him away. His heart raced, and his breath came in gasps. He stood absolutely still.

Gradually his pulse slowed. He remembered an old friend of his father's, a man who had spent his life hunting the bush. The old fellow had said, "When you're tracking, make sure nothing's tracking you." Jerry turned slowly, looking back the way he'd come. Almost a mile back, maybe a little more, he could see smoke still rising from the airbase. He tried to imagine what would've been going on. Sooner or later, probably sooner, the old man would have come out from behind the wreck of the helicopter and found Jerry missing. What would he do then? If he was smart, he'd do exactly what Jerry had done, and he would be somewhere back there in the bush. If he wasn't smart, he'd just sit down and wait for the soldiers to come back. When they said "Where's the other guy?" he'd say he didn't know. Then the soldiers would hit him. Very shortly, to get them to stop hitting him, he'd say "He was working over there." Then the soldiers would go look at the bodies, and they'd see Jerry's tracks heading away, out into the bush. What would they do then?

Perhaps they'd follow. But more likely, they'd just send somebody back to the shed where they found Jerry originally. When he wasn't there, and he certainly didn't plan on being there, then their actions would be less easy to predict. They might simply drop it. After all, as far as they knew he was just an Igbo refugee who'd taken French leave from a work detail. They'd probably not spend time looking for him in the city. If someone happened

47

to see him and recognize him, they'd pick him up, and then things would be very bad indeed. But unless they started rounding up Igbos in general, he should be safe enough for a day or so with a change of clothes and a change of address. Clearly, he needed to get back into the town, improve his appearance slightly, and mingle.

Encouraged by having worked through the options and risks, he popped up again and looked north, trying to identify a place where he could sneak safely back into town. Straight ahead were the backs of houses where there would be barking dogs and potentially hostile people. But a bit further west, the bush transitioned into a couple of plowed fields, and beyond them were what appeared to be warehouses. Jerry concluded that a disheveled and unwashed individual coming in from the fields would be less conspicuous than the same person walking up behind somebody's house. He started moving again.

It took another thirty minutes. When he got to the edge of the field, he did a very careful examination of everything he could see. There was no one in sight, no one working the fields, no one coming and going. What he hadn't realized was the effect that the attack on the airfield would have had on the population. Ibos had seen the government troops running randomly around and decided that the best plan was to stay inside, doors closed, shutters latched. Hausa and Fulani residents had also seen the troops, heard the explosions, and seen the smoke from the airbase; they decided to keep their heads down until it was clear who was fighting and who was winning. Naturally, Jerry didn't know this. All he could see was deserted fields and a bit of the town with nothing whatsoever going on. If there was no one to blend in with, his chances of being spotted seemed much greater. Reluctantly he decided he was going to have to wait it out; he was going to have to crouch here in the scrub until at least twilight, preferably until dark.

... come to the window ...

On Thursday morning, June thirteenthth, Jenn called MacArthur while she was finishing breakfast. For her, breakfast was usually perfunctory, and today it was even more so. She'd come home late the night before after squaring away the Kirk murder case (to the extent it could be squared away in one evening.) She'd spent another forty-five minutes giving brief attention to the other things that were on her plate and finally left the office at eleven-thirty. She ate a small quantity of leftovers for dinner and tried with only limited success to go to bed. Sleep came hard, and this morning she was already late. Now, she was eating a bowl of some kind of cereal with a handful of nuts tossed in and trying to give MacArthur as much of a briefing as she could, given that she was running behind and he was running ahead; he was seldom up and communicating this early.

"So," she said, "it depends on the bullets. Connelly says the one in the floor is useless, but the one in the body can probably be matched."

"That's two," said Mac, "and the third one went out the wall and down the street. What about bullet number four?"

"I don't know where it went. If the device worked the way Connelly thinks, then it would be a lower angle. On the back wall. But there wasn't anything there."

"Any windows in the back wall?"

"Only in the back door itself. And they were all intact."

"So Louie Burke was on his way up there and ran into somebody?"

"He says somebody hit *him*."

"Ah," said Mac. He was not at his most charming. He usually tried to be nice to Jenn; in fact, he tried to be nice to people in general. But he'd actually had to get out of bed to answer this call, which meant he hadn't eaten yet, showered, nor had any coffee. His joints hurt, one leg in particular. His eyes were dry and scratchy, and he had a sore throat: typical morning symptoms among the post-transplant, suppressed-immune-system crowd. If he was allowed to get up on his own schedule, eat, take pills, shower and dress at a leisurely pace, and pour a substantial quantity of strong coffee into his system, he could be reasonably effective and moderately pleasant to deal with by, say, ten-thirty. This morning, though, he was feeling rushed and inconvenienced, and of course, Jenn hadn't bothered to call him yesterday when the body was discovered.

There was no reason why she should have, but he'd come to expect it. He recognized that he was being petty, and that just made him crankier.

"So," Jenn said, after a slightly uncomfortable pause, "I'm going back out there. Do you want to come and ..." she almost said "poke around," but she stopped herself, changing it to "take a look?"

"Well, not right this minute," Mac said. "I'd need to get ..." he almost said "dressed," but changed his mind. "My act together a bit more. How long will you be there?"

"Most of the day, I imagine. They're going to call me about the autopsy, and I got some help with tracking down next of kin, so I can spend as much time as I need to. Looking through his stuff, I mean."

"Okay. I'll just drive out there when I'm on my feet."

"Oh, I'm sorry, Mac. Did I get you out of bed?"

"No, no," he lied. "I just move a little slow the first thing. I have to eat something before I can ... take a pill." That last phrase was another quick change from "take my meds," a phrase he used often enough with Colleen and to himself. He didn't like the sound of it when he was talking to Jenn or to other cops, though. It had a psychotropic connotation that wasn't exactly flattering; the Department used to talk about people who were behaving irrationally as being off their meds.

"Fine, fine. Take your time. I'll tell the patrol kids to keep an eye out for you."

Jenn hung up and expended another sixty seconds sending a text message to Andy Patel: *call me when you're not driving*. She knew he'd be somewhere between his condominium and the Detroit FBI office at Michigan Avenue and Cass. It was on a long, bare block with just three undistinguished office towers, a bit east of the Celtic knot formed by the Fisher and John Lodge freeways. It wasn't a pleasant or relaxing commute from anywhere, let alone Andy's place, and the last thing she wanted to do was distract him while he was dodging semis, road-enraged mortgage bankers, and Detroit police cars. Time enough to talk when he'd gotten into the office, checked his calendar, and had his stand-up with his boss.

In fact, Andy'd gotten an earlier start than usual, and he was walking in from his parking space when he got Jenn's message. When he called her, therefore, she was still on her way to the crime scene. Unusually for two points in Ann Arbor, the actual route from her house—Miller into town and then back out again on Beakes and Plymouth Road—wasn't absurdly longer than a straight line; it was six miles, give or take, and the crow-flies distance was a little more than four and a half. Further, since it was still early June, the annual festival of road repair had yet to shut the city down. She pulled into a BP station to answer the call.

"Hi," she said. "That was quick."

"Yeah," Andy said, "I'm just walking into the building. What's up?"

"I just wanted to tell you. We got a victim on that weird device thing ... I think we do, anyway. Should know for sure today."

"No kidding? A homicide?"

"Yeah, he's dead all right. Just waiting to hear if it was one of the guns in the box that shot him."

"Odd, odd, odd business. Who is he?"

"He's a professor at the U. Was."

"Odder still. So are we still on for tonight?" There had been plans to eat and hear some music.

"Yes, if you're still up for it," she said. "I worked on this thing late yesterday, and I don't plan on doing the same today." A pause.

"Sure, it sounds great to me. I have to be out in the field most of the afternoon. So I might not get up there until, say, six-thirty? Is that still good?"

"That's fine. Do you want to meet downtown?"

"Frankly, I can find your house. I'm not sure I can find anything else in Ann Arbor."

"Great! My house at six or six-thirty, and then we'll carry on from there."

"All right. Well, um, carry on."

"Okay, bye."

Both parties disconnected, both felt slightly uncomfortable. Jenn wished she'd picked another term besides "carry on," Andy wished he hadn't automatically echoed it; it might have sounded as though he was mocking her. And the uncertainty of their friendship made things just a little awkward; *were* they carrying on? Not so far, they weren't, by any definition of the term. They'd seen each other socially just three times; tonight would be date number four, and this time it *was* unquestionably a date: dinner and some folk music. Neither of them was romantically predatory, neither of them was driven by a need to compete or reproduce. Jenn had all the children she could stand, Andy didn't want any to begin with. Actually, both were relatively content by themselves. But still: at least on Jenn's part, there was an attraction, if only because it struck her as so unlikely that she'd meet a cop who didn't appear to be a caveman. She'd divorced one of those already, after all, and never met anyone else even close to her age who appealed, cop or otherwise.

For Andy, it was complicated not by previous relationships (he'd never been married or even close to it) but by a piece of advice he'd gotten in his teens. His mother had told him, with regard to dealing with girls, "Just don't be pushy. Don't be a jerk about it." That was the extent of it, since neither of his parents were pushy, themselves. They gave little advice about anything, whether it was joining the Marines, leaving the Marines, or taking a job with the FBI. He would say "I think I'm going to do ..." and his mother and father would nod and say little or nothing. So when one of them actually suggested something, he took it seriously. He'd spent his time in college, his time in the Corps, and his career to date in the Bureau trying not to be a jerk about women.

When Mac turned onto Playwright Lane, he had no problem identifying the Kirk house. There were cars of various official kinds parked all over the place, and the whole lot was taped off. He parked well down the street and gave his well-practiced smile and 'no comment' head shake to the lone Fox reporter still hanging around. Nothing public had been said about the device, and without that aspect of the story, it was still just a one-shot, one-victim homicide, only unusual in that it was in Ann Arbor. The department's public affairs officer had given the press a few content-free sentences, and there'd been the usual video of police vehicles coming and going; unless something more lurid turned up, even the shooting of a faculty member would be edged off the top slot in the evening broadcast. Another mayor in yet another suburb was being encouraged to resign or at least step down for the duration of his federal racketeering trial, and his police chief, who *had* just resigned, was holding a press conference to explain why.

Jenn was inside the house with another detective, Larry Whitaker, working out a division of labor. Kirk's home office was lined with file cabinets, and they were trying to arrive at a logical way to divide them up. Whitaker was an old hand, almost as old as MacArthur, and he'd lost all his competitive reactions. He didn't care if Jenn ran the case or if Mac did or frankly if they put a K9 officer in charge. He'd take as big a pile of paperwork as Jenn wanted to hand off, haul it back to his desk, and happily tell that damn pushy real estate agent whose Audi had been broken into that the investigation would take a little longer now: "I'm working a homicide, you understand."

"Mister MacArthur," he said. "You returning to the scene of the crime?"

"If I did it, I wouldn't show up while they've got pros like you on the job."

"Hi, Mac," said Langton. "Feeling better?"

"Hey, MacArthur, investigate this, would ya?" said Whitaker. He was holding a box of correspondence in both hands at waist height, and he made a vaguely suggestive thrusting motion with it. "You worried about the government, at all?"

"The government? No, not ... usually. How do you mean?"

"Garage is full of subversive books," said Whitaker.

"Kirk was into spy stuff," said Jenn. "He wrote this." She held out a copy of a paperback: *Abandonné: The Lost Agents and Soldiers of Indochina,* by Alan G. Kirk, PhD. Mac checked the front matter quickly: 2009, University of Illinois Press. The back cover told him that it was the first scholarly work on the French government's callous abandonment of its operatives in Vietnam, Laos, and Cambodia. Apparently, when the effort against the Viet Minh fell apart, many soldiers, intelligence agents, and locals were left to be killed, captured, or to starve. Besides the brief summary of the book, there were the usual positive excerpts from reviews ("... carefully researched and presented with a convincing thoroughness ...", "Kirk has worked through a mass of newly-declassified material from both French and American agencies ..."). There was also a bit of author biography. It said that Dr. Kirk was an Assistant Professor of History at the University of Michigan, that he specialized in "the nascent global intelligence networks of the post-colonial period," and that *Abandonné* was his first book.

"There are five boxes of these in the garage," Jenn said.

"Not a best seller?"

Whitaker walked out the front door with his box of paper, headed for his car.

"Hard to say. Would you read it?"

"Actually, yes, "said Mac, "I would. But I don't think I know anybody else who would. Any sense of what all the documents are?"

"It's a mixed bag. There are some student things ... papers and exams. Meeting minutes and admin stuff. University documents. And then lots of correspondence. I guess you don't just text governments when you want classified information."

"Classified?"

"Yes. I just sampled a few documents, but it looks as though he spent a lot of time asking for access to things. Demanding it, sometimes."

"That's what Whitaker was talking about? Afraid of the government, did he say?"

"It's all pretty old. At least the sample I looked at. Fifties and Sixties and Seventies. Not like he was asking about Al-Qaeda."

"The Fifties and Sixties and Seventies," thought Mac. Post-colonial, for sure: the period when the British and the French and the Belgians were turning their backs and walking away from their colonies. Lots to be ashamed of, but nothing to murder an obscure American academic over. And sure as hell not with some ridiculous black powder booby trap.

"You don't think there's anything in that?" Mac asked.

"I don't think much of anything, yet," Jenn said. "There's too much of this stuff to get through. And I have to talk to the student who was looking for Kirk."

"And all the usuals: girlfriends, boyfriends, family, neighbors."

"Bosses, subordinates. I think I'll leave the CIA toward the bottom of the list."

"Not to mention the DGSE."

"The who?" said Jenn.

"French spooks. Directorate General of ... something Exterior. I don't even remember why I know that."

"Right. Do you ever forget anything?"

"I don't remember. Do you want me to go think about where that fourth bullet might have gone?"

"Have a ball. A ball, get it? I need to start making some phone calls."

Sixty miles east, more or less, Andy Patel closed the door of his immediate superior's office and walked down the hall toward his cubicle. In case anyone was watching, he gave it four or five steps to set a conceptual distance between the meeting he'd just had and the body language he desperately wanted to display. When he was safely outside some perceived zone of association with his boss, he shook his head, slowly, deliberately, and in a manner expressing deep disbelief.

Instead of giving the senior agent a quick summary of his current case— civic corruption in a suburb called Gardner— Andy had received a phone number and a task. "Call this woman in Washington, Patel, and see if you can help her find out what's going on in Ann Arbor. You know someone up there, right?"

"Yes, sir," Andy'd said, and he glanced at a slip of paper. It had a name, Divina San Martin, a phone number with a Virginia area code, and a single acronym: CIA.

... the cliffs of England stand ...

Should children be encouraged to dream? Is it better if they simply grow up with the same idiot stereotypes and myths as their peers? Do you do them any favor by reading to them, early on, and from books that will never be made into an epic mini-series or an online role-playing game? Belonwu Mbanugo would not have asked himself those questions; he was an engineer or intended to be, not a psychology major. But he was someone about whom they could be asked.

His father and his older sister read to him in his extreme youth, but not from children's books. They read him the books they liked themselves, mystery stories all the way back to Conan Doyle. By the time he was five, he was playing Hercule Poirot, translating himself into a suave Belgian detective, and turning the ruinous streets of Gardner into prewar England. But when he began to choose for himself from the dusty, ignored books in the grade school library, he found a new world, the strange parallel universe occupied by the characters of Arthur Henry Sarsfield Ward, a man who wrote as Sax Rohmer.

In Ward's clumsy and formulaic novels, the hero is a plaster cast of an English gentleman, Sir Denis Nayland Smith, who struggles against the treachery and malice of the lesser races, embodied in the form of Doctor

Fu Manchu, a Mandarin with an artificially lengthened life, a pet marmoset, and an army of assassins, poisoners, and treacherous young women, drawn from every non-white ethnic group Ward had ever heard of and some he made up. To describe his books as Eurocentric or in fact as flamingly racist would be to put it mildly.

Although Ward was English, the action in his books was global, and a surprising amount of it took place in America. It even came as close to home as Detroit's Shrine of the Little Flower, home of the infamous anti-Semitic Radio Priest, Father Charles Coughlin; he appears, thinly disguised, as a hero in one of the novels. Ward wrote quickly, and the plots were so similar, book to book, as to be laughable. They were just a framework on which he hung whatever menace he thought English-speaking readers would be afraid of, decade after decade: the Yellow Peril, economic collapse, the rise of Germany and Italy, the rise of the Soviet Union, the rise of *anybody*, frankly, who wasn't a straight-nosed, straight-talking, pipe-smoking, English-speaking white guy, with a weaker but still very Anglo-Saxon sidekick and a direct line to the Prime Minister.

What, in a body of rubbish like that, could possibly have appealed to a third-generation Igbo youth, growing up in a dying Detroit suburb at the end of the twentieth century? The villains, of course. Belonwu, as a boy, imagined himself not as the rigid and closeted Nayland Smith, but as one of Fu Manchu's lieutenants, a strong, loyal, dedicated member of the Si-Fan, Ward's imaginary international order of evil. Depending on which book you were reading, the all-powerful Doctor Fu Manchu either led the Si-Fan or served on its board of directors or was merely its humble servant. Regardless, the doctor's every move was intended to further the downfall of the west and to bring to the fore the Asian peoples and the African peoples of the Earth. (We hear little of India in Ward's books; presumably, some of his best friends were Hindu.)

In his games, Belonwu crept silently up to houses, inserting deadly jungle insects through windows or planting poisonous serpents disguised as walking sticks. He didn't long for a pet dog, he wanted a vicious Egyptian baboon to strangle enemies of the cause; he even had a scheme for keeping it healthy. (In Ward's universe, the baboon gave itself away by coughing, having been imported into England and, of course, catching cold. In Belonwu's imagination, his baboon would have had a sweater.)

He was not an exceptionally athletic or dexterous boy, himself, but in his private world, he employed those who were, giant Nubians with massive strength, Sea Dayaks from Sarawak who could tie knots no one else could undo, Japanese biochemists who could turn spider silk into cord no one could cut. For every frontal assault or simple-minded police raid his imaginary opponents mounted, he had a cunning and sophisticated counter attack or a plan of escape. It was a solitary game; his friends had no idea what he was talking about, when he was unwise enough to talk at all. He might as well have said "Let's play *Kidnapped*! You can be the Jacobites, and I'll be the Campbells!" None of the kids he knew had read Stevenson, let alone Sax Rohmer.

The game lasted until he was nine or ten, and even when he stopped acting on it, he retained a deep affection for murk and foggy nights and gas lamps. Plots and subterfuge were attractive notions. Without connecting it with his childhood enthusiasms, he collected old movies and TV series episodes; he saw all the old Sherlock Holmes stories with Jeremy Brett and all the Poirot tales with David Suchet. Then, in his early teens, he heard obliquely about kids who dressed in a kind of filtered Victorian way, boys who carried canes and wore top hats. As a high school junior, he met some people who had this enthusiasm, and they took him to a gathering in Dearborn. For the first time, he heard the term 'Steampunk'.

... the world, which seems to lie before us...

Jerry Mbanugo was tired, tired, tired. He lay on a mattress on the floor and tried to sort out the situation. He remembered the walk (skulk might be a better term) through Enugu, imagining government patrols or hostile mobs around every corner. He'd dodged a mixed bag of police, one small group of apparently drunken government troops, and an equally small band of Hausa civilians, armed with sticks and chanting, "*A raba!*" (Let us separate!) He remembered his huge relief when his knock on the door of a specific house was answered. His only plan had to been get off the street, change clothes perhaps, and rest. The things that had happened subsequently, though, were only dimly understood. In his state of mental and physical exhaustion, he was now letting events move him along.

Jerry had never had any training in tradecraft. He was not an agent in any real sense, and he had no vocabulary of espionage to rely on. As he made his way through Enugu's streets and alleys, he'd pondered what he'd say if he actually managed to connect with someone from his employer, and he concluded that a full account of the day wouldn't reflect all that well on himself. He'd done nothing useful, really, and by running out on the soldiers, he'd brought himself to their attention. He didn't know the phrase 'My cover is blown' in English, Igbo, or any other language, and so when the man at the door let him in and asked "What is it?" Jerry just said, "They know who I am."

To Jerry's surprise, the man didn't seem surprised. Instead, he led Jerry back to a small room and brought him new, western-style clothes. Tea and food came next, and then his host brought out a notebook.

"What name?" he asked.

Jerry just stared at him. "What name you use?" the man said again, speaking in English. Startled, Jerry told him, "Jerry Mbanugo," and spelled it. The man wrote it out and left the room. He stuck his head back in the door and said, "Be ready one hour."

What it was that he was to be ready for, Jerry didn't know, and he was too tired to care. He rolled his old clothes up into a ball for a pillow and as he did so, felt a bulge in one pocket. He took out the dead officer's money and slipped it into the new pants he was wearing. Then he opened the small envelope.

He had never seen uncut diamonds before, but even in his mental state, the deduction wasn't difficult. There were a dozen of them, raw but partly translucent, mostly clear with one blue stone and one slightly yellow. None was smaller than a quarter-inch across.

Sheer terror. Panic. He should never have touched that man, that officer, that devil incarnate! They would know! Someone would know what he had in that envelope! Someone would be looking for it! They would ask the soldiers, and the soldiers would know who they left there to clean up! Jerry wanted the diamonds *away*, away from him, out of his possession! He stared wildly around the room, looking frantically for a hiding place.

In one corner, a bullet or a shell fragment or some other accident of the government assault on Enugu had left the wall slightly broken. A gap like a cartoon mouse hole existed at the point where the wall touched the floor. Jerry wrapped the envelope around the stones tightly, making a cylinder out of it, and slipped it into the hole, then off to the left into the hollow cavity between two displaced mud bricks. He rocked back on his knees, brushed away the marks in the dust, and felt just marginally better. He went back to the mattress and lay down again.

He didn't make it to sleep. Suddenly, the man was back, carrying a suitcase. "They here," he said.

"Who? Who's here!?" Jerry gasped, speaking Igbo in his consternation.

"You talk English," said the man. "You go now. Here." He gave Jerry the suitcase. "You take this, too."

Jerry was utterly confused; 'this' was a passport, astonishingly, a United States passport. He flipped it open; it showed a poorly-focused photo of some young African man, and the name read 'Jerry Mbanugo'.

He let the man lead him to the front door. He had no plan, no reaction. Events moved him along, like being pushed by the wind, like moving in a dream. At the door was a white man in a suit; he said nothing, just took the suitcase from Jerry and stepped back outside. There was a car with an African in the driver's seat. Jerry stayed awake for twenty minutes or so of the ride, but after that he fell asleep. When he woke up, it was at an airfield, somewhere. The American led him into a small building and left him with a group of five other men. No one said anything; they sat on benches and waited. After an hour, two new men, speaking English with French accents, came and asked for passports. Jerry showed them his strange new credentials, and along with the others, walked out onto a runway. They went up a set of boarding stairs and chose seats in an empty plane. It was May twenty-third, 1969.

Thirty-four hours later, Jerry, by now alone, was in a hotel in Detroit. Forty-eight hours after that, a man in northern Virginia was trying to sort out how his overseas colleagues had extracted the wrong person from Enugu.

... also in the sound a thought ...

Mats had been strategically placed on the garage floor, making lanes where cops and medical examiners and other official persons could walk without buggering up the crime scene. By now, noon on Thursday the thirteenth, Kirk's body was gone, his possessions were slowly being catalogued and some hauled away, and everything had been photographed. Mac stood on one of the mats, close to the spot where the device had probably been, and stared at the walls. He tried to imagine Kirk discovering the device. He'd come home, opened his garage door, and seen something in the way. He'd walked in, examined it, and picked it up. And it had shot him. Then—or certainly shortly afterwards—it had fired three more times. In the garage, the shots would have been loud, amplified. Kirk probably yelled or screamed. The door would have been wide open, broadcasting the sound toward the west and across the street. No one had heard anything, though. Why not?

Mac looked up at the ceiling; nothing was attached to the exposed rafters except a pair of bare-bulb light sockets. Specifically, there was no electric garage door opener. He modified his narrative to match that fact: Kirk had come home, gotten out of the car, and manually opened the garage. Did that matter? Mac looked at the inside of the door and saw a lock mechanism near the bottom, a pair of rods connected by a crank. They looked as though they were in the locked position, sticking through holes in the door edge and into the frame. Mac's first house had had a lock of that type; outside, there'd be a handle with a key. You unlocked it, turned the handle, and the rods retracted, letting you raise the door by hand. The door was now and apparently had been closed. So either Kirk didn't open it himself, or he did and then someone closed it again. Who? Well, most likely the person who came back to get the device. And that would most likely be the person who left it in the first place.

Someone had come in the garage's back door, too, probably. The patrol officer, Jeri Klein, had found it open, and someone else had reported signs of it having been opened with a thin blade. That was probably how the device came in and maybe how it left. There was a row of mats leading toward that back door, and Mac followed it out into the yard, looking carefully at the door jamb and the cheap knob lock; he agreed that it had probably been forced open. He went on around to the front of the house, knocking honeysuckle leaves onto the brim of his cap. A tow truck was in the process of hooking up the Honda, getting it ready for a trip to a department garage where it could be examined methodically.

"How's it going?" he asked the tow driver. "You have to pop the doors on the car?"

"Okay. How's it goin'?" repeated the driver. "Nah, it was unlocked."

"Huh," said Mac. There were still people who left their cars unlocked, but it was more of a student habit than something an adult would do. He knelt down at the garage door and looked closely at the chrome handle. As he'd expected, it had a key socket; Mac pulled his hand back into his sleeve and with this makeshift glove, cautiously tried to turn the handle. It didn't move. Locked or jammed; Mac thought of that jimmied back door lock and wondered if someone had tried to force this one, too, maybe failed to get it open. He looked at it again, swore slightly, and brought out his keychain light. Another look, this time using the flashlight, and Mac swore again and more explicitly. The keyhole was full of a transparent, glossy material, probably glue of some kind. Someone had ensured that this door couldn't be opened easily.

Back inside the garage, Mac thought about the fourth bullet. He took Jenn's statement for granted that there was no visible hole for it. After all, he'd taught her how to look at a crime scene; if she couldn't see it, he wouldn't be able to, either. "*So assume there's no hole in a wall or a window,*" he thought; "*if that fourth round did fire in here, where the hell else could it go? Not into a wall, not into a window ... ah! Walls, windows, doors!*" He was looking east, at the back of the garage, and there was that back door, standing open! He'd walked through it twice himself already. What might be straight out that door?

62

He stood in the doorway and looked east, imagining the device slipping out of Kirk's hands, that demonic pendulum swinging around, the fourth gun's hammer falling on a percussion cap, the barrel pointed just slightly downward—and the bullet hitting a fifty-year-old maple tree just about at the height of a human knee. He could see the mark from where he was standing, a slightly lighter colored dimple in the bark, offset to the right. He almost ran to the tree (Mac never *really* ran anywhere, any more), pulling out the flashlight again as he went. Yes, indeed! A fresh hole, splinters, and inside, the dull metallic color of deformed lead. Four shots accounted for.

... by this distant northern sea ...

Until Achilles Gordon was twenty-eight, he'd never had a job that required actual work. Instead, he got paid (rather well, for a kid with no high school diploma) for standing around road construction sites with a reflective vest and a stop/slow sign. Ethnically, he was Greek and African-American, his mother's maiden name being Aristopolous. His father was a local politician in the city of Gardner, up to his eyebrows in the backstairs politics of the place, and it was trivial for him to place his unpromising son in jobs with paving contractors who owed favors. It took Achilles a long time (until, as noted, his late twenties) to realize that just collecting a pay check was essentially leaving money on the table. He consulted with his father, and the result was a move into a supervisor job at the city's Public Works Department. In addition to a pay check, small, unrecorded, tax-free amounts began to come his way. Doing business with the city had become a pay-to-play situation, and although the individual payments were small, almost everyone was getting something out of it.

Twenty years went by. His father had a heart attack and passed on. His mother took most of the estate's cash and went back to Kato Achaia on the north coast of the Peloponnese. Achilles stayed in Gardner, living in the family house and moving from job to job within the city government. He still did nothing much in the way of physical work, but his responsibilities multiplied. Now, on his forty-eighth birthday, he was in charge of the parking enforcement department; he had three people in the office and a dozen more on two shifts, writing parking tickets and calling for tow trucks. Officially, Achilles' job was to hire and fire, train the parking officers, and keep the towing contractors in line. In reality, it was a more complicated set of tasks.

The mayor of Gardner was a gentleman named Dougal Polowski. His nickname, for reasons no one could remember, was Scootch, and he had been first elected as mayor in 1994. There were no term limits in Gardner, and Scootch was re-elected every four years smoothly and predictably. He was a Republican, himself, presiding over a city council with a Democratic majority, but there was no conflict along party lines. Party membership was little more than a way of financing campaigns, of getting money from the state organization with which to pay for ads and lawn signs and fliers. Instead, on the rare occasions when the city government disagreed on something, it split sharply between those who were loyal to the mayor and those who weren't. And the latter group were almost always those who had been excluded or thought they had been from one or more flows of illicit cash.

Scootch Polowski was perhaps not a strategic genius. His chances of rising from the mayoralty of a small, poor, chronically depressed city to anything higher—even the State House—were essentially zero. But he did have a kind of tactical shrewdness. He was smart enough to see that the role of big frog in a small, stagnant pond was not so much a stepping stone to greatness as it was a living, and a living that in his own private words, "Sure beats workin'." He was acutely aware that sixty or seventy percent of his personal income was illegal and that his business methods were likewise. He knew that there were city employees, many of them, on the payroll whose official, taxable salaries were less than that of a new hire at a fast food restaurant; somehow those people supported families, paid mortgages on their homes, and sent their children to college. Sometimes the mayor would wake up at four o'clock in the morning and wonder what life would be like in a federal prison. But he comforted himself, as did many of his employees, colleagues, and vendors, with the thought that Gardner and its peculations were small potatoes, far too little to interest the authorities, the media, or even the run of the mill citizen—not with the corruption circus going on just to the east, over in Detroit.

And so over the years, the job of being the mayor became something like running a small business. Traditional sources of revenue were taken for granted and considered to be products running out of steam. Property taxes were assumed to be in a state of permanent decline. State and federal funds were free money, but they were also the subject of intense competition among hundreds of similar small cities, and many of them had a lot more clout in Lansing and Washington than poor old Gardner. Of the thirty-four thousand people living in the city, not one outside Polowski and his circle of associates had ever been elected to anything; few could even name their state and federal representatives. There were no influential businessmen with state-level juice because there were no businesses in Gardner that mattered much outside the city limits. Consequently, other sources had to be found, other cash flows identified. Once, five or six years back, a very small group of concerned citizens proposed a city income tax; Council's interest in that proposal could best be described as less than none.

Some of the other sources were traditional and time-honored. Even a cash-strapped city had to buy things, and Gardner was no exception. A contract to do asphalt work, for example, might cost the city a hundred and eighty-five thousand dollars in terms of the check it wrote to the contractor, but there would be a corresponding flow of money, favors, simple-minded employment, and outright gifts from the contractor back to city officials. Of course, the asphalt guys would have to find ways to recoup their losses, and perhaps the actual work performed and materials supplied might not be particularly good. But of course, that just meant more work to be done, a few years down the road.

Licenses and permits were another common product area. It required careful management to ensure that doing business within the city wasn't so expensive that owners would simply choose not to. But moving a business is itself expensive, and the longer it was open and the more entrenched a place became, the more often it might be inspected. If the outcome of that inspection was more dependent on the relationship with the city than it was on compliance, well, that's business, isn't it?

And then, of course, there was law enforcement. The wonderful thing about a municipal police force is that, within the bounds of reason, it's a legal means by which a city can force people to hand over money. Obviously, local cops have to spend a certain amount of their time dealing with real crime and real criminals, but those tend to be unprofitable operations. Traffic tickets and parking tickets, on the other hand, can be made to pay. Reduced to its most simple terms, the business proposition is just this: we say you broke the law. You can spend your time and money fighting us about it, or you can put a hundred and twenty-five dollars on your credit card, and it'll all go away. Which would you like to do? In a sense, it's like a casino; a calculated percentage of the time, the customers lose, and the odds favor the house.

Still, in a town as small as Gardner and one that had relatively little to draw non-resident traffic, there was only so much that could be gleaned. There weren't as many customers in the casino as there needed to be. It was this shortcoming of the traffic game that Polowski set out to remedy. One morning in 2002, a city department manager dropped by and asked to call in a favor; his mother had been stopped for speeding, and he wanted the whole thing fixed: no points on her license, no fine, no court date. The mayor, in gratitude for whatever it was this guy had done for him last month (he honestly didn't remember), wasted a phone call and a whole five minutes of his valuable time making the speeding ticket vanish.

Now, though, the guy owed *him*. Just as much as if he'd gotten his nephew a job or had potholes on his street filled in, this guy now owed his old pal, Scootch, in the barter currency of patronage, for one fixed traffic ticket. Was there something there? A seedling of an idea? Could this kind of reciprocity be made formal and even accountable-for?

The next morning around four am, Polowski woke up. A dream or acid reflux or something put an end to sleep, and immediately the worries set in. This was an old pattern, and he usually tried to counter it by thinking of other things, things he could actually control. This particular morning, he started to think about traffic tickets, and instantly he realized why fixing them annoyed him. There was no money in it. The city lost a few dollars of revenue in the form of fines, and the mayor got nothing but political capital out of it. Right now, he had as much of that as he needed; what he'd rather have was a few thousand dollars more a year. Plus, he thought, there were costs. Every time somebody wanted this elementary kind of favor, he had to pick up the phone, argue with somebody else, pull rank. It left a paper trail, too. If a ticket was written and then disappeared like an Argentine dissident, it could conceivably be discovered by somebody, sometime. Some damn journalist or an auditor or someone like that. If a ticket was written ...

No! The way to do this, he realized in a flash of insight, was to stop it ever happening in the first place. No special requests, no phone calls, no paper trails: the cops and the parking guys worked for him, didn't they? What if they had a list of people *not* to ticket in the first place? What if the mayor offered a kind of insurance policy?

Lying there beside his sleeping wife, Polowski thought it through. It was obviously illegal, but if the list was digital, stored on just one computer somewhere, it'd be easy to erase. Maybe even encrypt; the head of the city's IT group would know how to do that. And if the cops and meter maids were just told to call in license plates before they did anything and to back off if they got a certain kind of response, then that's all they'd have to know about it. Somebody would have to be in charge of managing the list, adding to it, taking people off it. Ah, Gordon over in the traffic department. He was already crooked in a number of ways. This would be just one more. So maybe this could be done with just three people who really knew what was up: his honor, the mayor; the IT guy; and Achilles Gordon. And that meant the fees would only be split three ways, too. That was good, especially since the mayor planned on executing the sales and the collection processes himself.

Eleven years later, the insurance business was just another part of Gardner's ongoing operations. Achilles Gordon had a personally-owned laptop, paid for by the city in ways not recorded on any set of books. It spent its life in the top drawer of a locked file cabinet, and it was connected to the Police Department's office network by an ethernet cable running out a hole in the back. The IT manager backed it up periodically, to a USB hard drive that *he* personally owned and that lived in a locked cabinet in *his* office. He took the drive home with him at night.

When a patrol officer observed a traffic infraction, he called in the license plate. Before a parking officer wrote a ticket, he made a similar call. The dispatchers did all the normal things—checking to see if the car was on any stolen lists, associated with any felonies, and so on—and they also checked it against a simple database running on Gordon's laptop. If the plate was found, the dispatcher would see nothing more unusual than the license number with the letter 'I' appended. Dispatch would read the number back to the officer, with or without the 'I' suffix, and if the 'I' was there, the officer would back off. There were several theories among the rank and file concerning what 'I' meant; some thought it was 'important' as in VIP. Others said no, it stood for 'interest', as in a person of interest in an investigation. No one except the mayor, the IT manager, and Gordon knew that it really meant 'insured'.

Unfortunately, there was a flaw in the design of the database. None of the people involved in creating it were especially well-qualified information architects. The assumption had been that insurance would be purchased by drivers or owners of individual cars with specific license plates. They didn't think about a business owner who might want to 'insure' a block of meters in front of his pawn shop or a church that might want parking restrictions relaxed on Sundays. And it certainly didn't take into account the bar owner who wanted to make sure his customers weren't targeted for DUI enforcement. So these special cases were handled separately, via word of mouth. Officers of any kind working specific areas were verbally instructed on the places to avoid, and they were encouraged not to ask questions. Occasionally, outstanding performance in looking another way would receive a small monetary reward. This whole side procedure, this group insurance plan, had started as a couple of exceptions and gradually expanded to take up a substantial amount of time, even as it generated a welcome increase in revenue.

The main problem was the need for enforcement personnel to keep the boundaries and terms of the insured areas in mind. Although the actual, academy-trained police officers weren't substantially better or worse than those in other small cities, the parking officers were, to put it in Achilles Gordon's words, a crew of idiots. They seemed incapable of grasping the meaning of simple instructions, things like "Don't write citations on the six hundred block of Crown Street." Reverend Sam of the Glory and Credit Full Jesus Church wanted his parishioners to enjoy free parking, and he was willing to pay for it. But nobody wanted that sort of arrangement written down, so making it happen depended on the long-term memory of twelve men and women who had their jobs in the parking force for much the same reason that most city employees were employed: favors. They were neither motivated nor dedicated.

This sort of thing could cause at least two kinds of problems for Achilles. The more common occurred when a parking officer forgot instructions, wandered onto Crown Street on a Sunday, and wrote a bunch of tickets. Shortly afterward, Achilles' phone would ring, and he'd have to placate the Reverend Sam or one of his deacons. Then he'd have to track down the tickets in question and make them vanish. And then he'd have to conduct some remedial training for a cranky, ungrateful, underpaid meter person.

The other problem came about when the process worked but worked too well. Some resident of Crown Street would become unhappy with all the church parking. Or someone who lived next to Uncle Bob's Grill got tired of drunks roaring up and down the street, in cars or not. These aggrieved citizens would usually call the police, and the police, since they knew perfectly well that Uncle Bob's was owned by a special friend of the city, would proceed slowly.

Step one would be to send an officer to investigate. That would typically happen much later, say, a couple of hours after closing time. If there was still any roaring going on at that hour, it probably *should* be gently discouraged. After all, Uncle Bob could be reminded that he had the no-DUI policy but not the mayhem rider. Mostly, though, all would be quiet, and the officer could report that no lawbreaking had been observed. In many cases, this would be sufficient to put the complaint to rest.

If the citizens persisted, step two would be to contact Uncle Bob or Reverend Sam and let them know that there had been complaints. This conversation would include specific identification of the unhappy parties. Then, Uncle Bob and his attorney or the Reverend and a few deacons could pay a polite visit to the complainant and discuss the matter. After a frank exchange of views, the complaint would almost always be withdrawn. This latter sort of problem didn't touch Achilles except in the aftermath, when he'd have to credit Uncle Bob's account and extend the period of coverage for another year. It was very much like running a customer service group; it was certain that problems would occur, and the task was to close them out at minimal cost to the enterprise and without losing a client. It was a job that generated stomach acid.

Charles Blake also had stomach trouble. He was a white guy from the north suburbs, trying to be a businessman for some definition of the term. He wasn't very good at it; his big idea was a chain of car washes, located where he could get the land to build on or where he could buy an existing place. He'd started with a small amount of seed money from his parents and bolstered it during the housing bubble by the old routine of buying, renovating, and flipping existing homes. That was more physical work than he was interested in doing, and he took his profits (lucky timing, there) and got out before the 2008 collapse. He built a car wash in Warren, bought one in Sterling Heights, and had his eye on the wealthier western suburbs (maybe even Livonia!) when another operator offered him a deal on a place in Gardner. It came at a good price in terms of the actual sale, and Blake wasn't quite smart enough to look into the hidden costs of doing business in a city like Gardner. He was being asked to pay twice as much for permits as he was used to, he was finding the various inspections onerous and bordering on extortionate, and he considered the city in general to be run by arrogant little bureaucrats. He still hadn't got the shop open, and he was running out of money. He had other things on his mind, too; he was getting married.

His fiancée, oddly enough, was herself from Gardner. He met her through one of his employees; she was tall, dark-skinned, charming if somewhat submissive. Her name was Akunna Mbanugo ('Her Father's Wealth'). She was the granddaughter of Jerry Mbanugo. She had a younger brother named Belonwu.

... like the folds of a bright girdle ...

Jerry Mbanugo had never heard of Detroit, except briefly in an economics class. He knew, once he'd slept off the jet lag, that he was in America. After looking frantically through the brochures and promotional magazines in his hotel room, he internalized the idea that Detroit was in a state called Michigan; he even found a map of the US. Besides knowing to within a few dozen miles where he was, he knew that some world-ranging power had gotten him out of danger in Nigeria and brought him here. He didn't know why; he didn't know that he was where he was because the man who should have knocked on the door of that safe house in Enugu had listed Detroit as his home city. Jerry was in a hotel because according to policy, those extracted from foreign assignments shouldn't just show up on their relatives' doorsteps without warning. After all, those relatives might not have known that their husband or son or cousin with the nice government job was even out of the country. Their employer would want to have some time to hear their report and remind them of what they could and couldn't say. So Jerry got to spend his first few days in the States keeping his head down. He spoke twice, briefly, with a man in a suit; the first conversation was extremely confused. After it became apparent to Jerry that some kind of mistake had been made and even more apparent to the local Agency man that far beyond a mistake, an absolute fiasco had occurred, he gave Jerry some cash and told him to sit tight.

If you've ever been part of a large organization, you can imagine for yourself the process that took place within the Agency. First, it had to be determined how much would be said internally. A small circle of people formed, informally, to define the real story and the official one; needless to say, the two would diverge widely. Next, those who knew embarrassing things but were not part of the circle had to be instructed (in some cases) or encouraged (in others) to adhere to the official story. As it emerged, the official story was that the other man, the person who was supposed to be extracted, had never shown up. He was presumed to be captured or dead. Jerry, the man who had actually been yanked out of Africa and dropped in Detroit, would be reconstructed as an actual, full-fledged agent, and there would be reasons invented for having pulled him out. Jerry himself and these reasons were hinted at in a couple of backdated documents. Of course, all of this was entirely for the internal purposes of the Agency itself; nothing about it was for the public or even the public's elected officials.

Two days later, Jerry had another chat with his new contact. His head was spinning by the time it was over, but he grasped that keeping quiet about Nigeria was essential; that Detroit was a good place for him now; that he had a bank account and that it would have funds deposited periodically; and that he should begin looking for a place to rent and, eventually, a job.

The man's parting comment was that the checking account had some extra funds to get things off the ground; he should buy some new clothes and a car.

For someone who had been summarily jerked out of a civil war in post-colonial Africa and tossed headfirst into a Midwestern American city, Jerry wasn't completely unprepared. He spoke rather good English, although with an odd blend of London and Igbo accents. He had the equivalent of a bachelor's degree in business, he was young and relatively healthy, and he had the very rare experience of playing a long-running role: living for months in Enugu as an illiterate refugee. But he had one severe deficit in the context of America: he'd never driven a car in his life. At home with his parents, he'd had a motorbike, but it was nothing more than a bicycle with a tiny engine. And the traffic situation there was anarchic, anyway. He knew, vaguely, that western countries had complicated driving rules and regulations, but he'd never imagined that he'd need to know anything about them. And buying a car? It had never crossed his mind.

He expressed this uncertainty to his visitor. The man appeared startled, but he accepted it as just another aspect of this colossal foul-up. "Well, then," he said, "I guess we'll have to sign you up for some driving lessons." There was a pause. "And when you get around to buying a car, maybe you should call me." He imagined Jerry and a used car dealer together and decided that the Agency wasn't going to get out of this quite as easily as perhaps it thought.

It took about a year, all told, for Jerry to work his way into his new life. Going to Enugu and leaving his family behind had been a wrench (the family is an important thing to an Igbo). But that initial separation had in some small way prepared him for this total one. After a few months, he began to accept that Nigeria was dead to him. He learned to drive; at least he didn't have to break the habit of driving on the left, since he'd never done it. He bought the smallest, least expensive used car he could, given the advice of his contact man. It was a 1965 Dodge Dart (the CIA man was a MoPar enthusiast). Its bronze paint was fading to a dull beige, and there was some evidence that the prior owner had also owned dogs. He looked at cheaper cars, but his mentor explained the concepts of rust and poor design and the effects of poor maintenance, and the clincher was the description of the horror should some heap break down on him in the middle of the night. Jerry was not clear exactly what dangers that would involve, but he agreed not to explore them. He passed up a 1964 Falcon and bought the Dart.

The spring of 1969 faded, as springs do, into summer. Jerry was fully involved now in a search for a job, and eventually he found one. His Agency friend coached him in applications and the mechanics of entry-level jobs, and they pondered what qualifications his education gave him. They decided that it would be better for him to start with blue-collar positions and go from there, rather than try to explain how a business degree from England would map to American requirements. Fortunately, at the tail end of the sixties, there were still well-paying union jobs to be had. In the thick shell of development around Detroit, there were hundreds of small, privately-owned machine shops and little manufacturing operations, scattered up and down Eight Mile Road and Lasher, Telegraph and Dequindre, Warren and Ford Road, McNichols and the Southfield. Jerry was hired, after a few rejections, by a family-owned place that made custom fasteners for Ford and Chrysler. They had a concrete block building in Dearborn, right on Michigan Avenue where it hits Telegraph.

It was almost a completely straight transaction. They had open jobs, and Jerry had the rather minimal qualifications. The only real help he got was a roundabout set of phone calls. The little plant had one government deal (not hugely profitable) acting as a subcontractor. The firm they supplied was a very large one, located in Warren, and they built very large, expensive things for the military. Jerry's friend called a friend of his at the Department of the Army, who called a program manager somewhere else, who called the owner of the little plant in Dearborn. All he said was that he'd heard of a guy, Jerry—he spelled the last name—who was smart and reliable and looking for a job. The owner found Jerry's application, called him and talked to him for a few minutes, and closed the deal.

In this kind of work, you hired a few genuine tradesmen, journeymen or actual master machinists, and you pretty much assumed that anyone other than that would need training. Jerry did, certainly, but he caught on quickly. On the job, he stood out, partly because of his accent and partly because he appeared to have no life outside work. He was always willing to put in overtime, and he never seemed to complain. Unlike the majority of the people hired off the street, he could *read*, for God's sake. So when one of the supervisors quit, instead of going outside, the plant owner asked Jerry if he'd like to step up. It would mean being out of the union, the boss pointed out, but he listed the compensations. Jerry listened silently, as he usually did, and then simply said, "Yes. Thank you. I will." It was the winter of 1971.

Jerry had been renting an apartment in Detroit, but with his new job, he nerved himself and bought a house. He was, actually, quite well off, at least by his standards. He had minimal expenses, his tastes were not rich, and there was no one he needed to impress. He figured out the difference in fuel and the wear and tear on his car, and he discovered that an inexpensive house with a shorter commute would be the better choice. Dearborn he found to be a bit above his price range, but right down the road was another city, a place called Gardner, and the houses there were much more attractively priced. He bought a nine hundred square foot cottage, and moved his small set of belongings in. It was a good decision, not only from an economic standpoint but also because it spared him, a single black man with a Nigerian accent, from finding out what it would have been like to try buying a house in Dearborn.

... the light gleams and is gone ...

Divina San Martin was looking at a pair of news stories, filtered for her by a simple-minded piece of software, drawn from a vast fire hose of digital information, mostly news feeds. For her, there were seldom more than one or two items, and frequently they were all irrelevant, false hits on names that happened to coincide with people of interest to her. Regardless, every morning and afternoon she checked the feeds, seeing whether any of them related to a list of fifty or so people. These were people in her assigned areas who had requested information from the CIA.

One of today's two stories was irrelevant, the other more than usually interesting. There could hardly be more than one Alan Kirk, Assistant Professor at the University of Michigan. He was on her list as having requested a large number of documents from the Sixties and Seventies, most recently about Nigeria. He was persistent; when his requests were turned down, he usually appealed, sometimes asking members of Congress to apply pressure. Now, according to a story in the Detroit Free Press, he'd just been murdered.

From San Martin's standpoint, this was not a good thing. Whatever agency was going to be looking into his death would probably link him with his requests, and if they were smart cops, they'd want to know what he'd been working on, who or what he'd been asking about, and a whole list of other questions. If any of those questions came her way, she wanted to be clear on what her answers should be, so she immediately called her boss. Of course, he knew nothing whatsoever about the Ann Arbor Police Department, but he did know people in the Detroit FBI office. If there were going to be questions, he'd prefer that he and his group got to handle them, and so in order to get Divina out ahead of the situation, he gave her a name 'up there' to call. Thus, at about eight forty-five, she got a return call from Andy Patel.

Among his other skills, Andy was good at listening, making positive noises, and providing noncommittal answers. He'd learned the method in college, polished it in the Marines, and found it highly valuable within the FBI. A musician might have said 'faking it'; Andy didn't have a name for it, but he put it into play whenever he wanted to seem helpful and cooperative without actually having much to say. In this case, he might have said to Ms. San Martin, "*I have no information on that, but I'll see what I can find out.*" Instead, the conversation was longer than that, substantially longer.

"Information Release. This is Agent San Martin."

"Yes, Ms. San Martin. My name is Andy Patel. I'm an Agent in the Detroit FBI office. I understand you're looking for information on a homicide in Ann Arbor?"

"Oh, yes. Thank you for the call, Agent Patel."

"Not at all. What can I help you with?"

"Well, I have some public information here related to a killing at the University of Michigan." Translated, this meant *I saw something in the news.*

"I see," said Andy. "Can you be a bit more specific? Is there a name of the alleged victim, for example?" In plain English, *There's a homicide approximately once a day in Southeastern Michigan. Any particular one?*

"Yes," she said. "A faculty member. Alan Kirk. Apparently shot."

"I'm aware of that case." This was strictly true since Jenn had told him about it a few minutes before. "The Bureau isn't involved, at least at this point. The local police are handling it." *So why are we having this conversation?*

"Professor Kirk had been in contact with us recently," Divina said. "So we're naturally concerned with his death." *Because my employer is even more averse to bad publicity than yours, pal.*

"Naturally. Have the local detectives been in touch with you?"

"No. I was hoping to determine whether there were any ... international aspects of their investigation." *Is there anything that connects him to spooky stuff?*

"In fact, you probably have more information, officially, than the Bureau does, right at this point," Andy said. He did his news reading in the evenings, and so if San Martin had even read a UPI story about Kirk, she knew more of the facts than he did. With a few exceptions. "But if it would be helpful to you, I could inquire informally with some personal contacts." *If I knew what you were fishing for, I could discuss it with the lead detective over dinner.*

"That would be very helpful, yes."

"Maybe you could give me a little more context, though, Agent San Martin," Andy said. "Are you concerned, for example, that the victim's ... I think you said *recent* ... contact with you might have a bearing on his death?" *Again, what are you looking for?*

76

"Is there any suggestion of that?" she countered.

"As I said, I don't have any details at all. But as I'm sure you'll agree, specific questions would be more likely to get answers." *Come on, lady. What do you want to know?*

"I can say ..." She paused, pretending to consider what she could reveal. The truth was that Kirk had simply requested access to some decades-old reports and memos, and only some scattered names and events within them were anything more than politically embarrassing now. She hadn't read them, wasn't interested in reading them, and didn't know why Kirk would want to. If it came down to comparing badges, her own clearance levels were probably lower than Andy's. She was a bureaucrat, responsible for handing out information that the agency was willing to hand out and for saying no when it was not willing. The genuinely classified knowledge she had was really just gossip and scandal, not matters of national security.

"I can say that Professor Kirk was doing historical research. His contact with us was solely as a requestor of information. And that information was related to ..." There was another pause, again for effect. "Events that took place prior to 1980."

"All right." *And so?*

"And so," she went on, "it would seem very unlikely that his professional activities were causal in anything like, ah, his death. If the investigating agency ..." she paused.

"The Ann Arbor Police Department," Andy said.

"Yes, the local police department. If they were to require input from us ... from the Agency ... we would of course cooperate in any manner, ah, concomitant with policy." *If anybody tells them anything, my department wants to do the telling.*

"Of course."

"So, we would be interested in making sure that they had access to the proper contacts." *I want them to call me, not go randomly poking around.*

"I think I understand," said Andy. "Would you have any problem with my putting them in touch with you, if they should ask for someone to speak to?" *And get out of the loop myself, so I can get some work done?*

"That would be acceptable," said Divina.

"I'm sure the detectives will be understanding. They're a very professional organization. The Detroit office has worked with Ann Arbor before, and we've been very impressed with their capabilities. And with their personnel." *In fact, I have a date with one of them tonight.*

"Well thank you very much, Agent Patel. I'll look forward to hearing from you."

Andy hung up, thinking how much time he'd had to waste, just to get San Martin to ask a concrete question. Obviously, she hoped he knew something useful about Kirk's murder, something like suspects, motives, whether the cops thought there was a government connection, and that he'd just spit it out. Officially, there was no reason he should have any such information. That he knew anything at all was a coincidence, and he allowed himself one quick moment of paranoia; he'd said nothing to anybody about seeing Jenn, but his boss had said, "You know someone up there, right?" That he'd worked with the Ann Arbor folks was well known; the Sturgis gunfight was legendary in the office. But maybe other details had leaked, too. No, he decided. The senior Agent just needed to get San Martin's call off his desk, and 'Ann Arbor' made him think of Andy. Nothing more.

He made a brief note of his phone call, sent his boss a message to the effect that he'd called the CIA and was looking into their concerns, and headed out of the office. He and another agent had an appointment, a meeting with an individual who wanted to talk about life and doing business in the city of Gardner.

On Thursday morning, Emily Weiden's alarm went off at its usual time, and she did get up, or partly up. Last night, she thought there'd be no sleep at all, but at last she'd managed it. Now, she sat on the side of the bed and looked at the wall, the window, the drawn curtains. Her apartment was small, one-fifth of a 1930s house; the interior walls had been repainted by the management company in some innocuous color, year after year. Emily hadn't brought much in the realm of decor when she came from Germany: an antique doll her mother had given her, a framed photo of the family, some books. It was a space to live in, even less connected with herself and her background than the student places she'd had in Europe. She was the fifty-first person to live in the apartment since the house was partitioned.

She let her head drop into her hands, elbows braced on knees, and felt— what *was* she feeling? Her eyes moistened slightly, but not enough to produce actual tears. Her weeping was over, and she didn't understand why there'd been any at all. Kirk was someone she hardly knew, nor could she have helped him if she'd gone looking for him any sooner. She didn't love him, she wasn't sure she'd even liked the man, she'd had little enough interaction with him. Then why this bleakness? Why was she so filled with a sense of loss? He was working with at least three other graduate students; were any of them so crushed by his death?

She tried to apply method to her questions. A thought experiment: what if another professor, say the woman in the next office from Kirk's, had been killed instead? Would she feel the same way? This was a person whose name Emily knew, someone she'd talked to on professional topics. If this woman had been shot to death in her home, in a sunny American suburb, what would Emily feel? She tried to be clinically honest with herself: she'd feel badly, of course. Sympathetic for the victim's family and students and friends. Frightened, a bit, just by the fact that it could happen. But not this same *loss*.

Emily's upbringing had been slightly on the dour side. Her father was a minister, her mother a psychologist, and she'd always been encouraged to *solve* problems, to see them in the light of right and wrong. When some gray area or shade of ambiguity prevented a black and white solution, her parents tended to step back to a cultural point of view: what was appropriate? What course of action would help keep a just society functioning and in balance? And if one still felt badly, well, why? Ask yourself why you feel the way you do.

She pulled on her running clothes, operating automatically; a run in the morning was a ritual for her. Sometimes it brought ideas, other days it only meant moving and breathing and dodging cars. Regardless, though, it always woke her fully and set a distance between the night and the morning. Today's morning, bright enough but still cool, helped clear her mind with the first few breaths. She went down the front steps of the house, stopped briefly to stretch, and then turned left away from the uninviting brick walls of a university sports complex, then left again on Dewey Street. The houses here were all older construction, partly student rentals, partly the homes of old residents or younger professionals. She ran past White Street, skipping the blasted landscape around the foot of the new Stadium Bridge. Instead, she kept on eastward, running by Cape Cods and Dutch Colonials, some with their original stucco or wooden siding, some with modern replacements. It wasn't Germany nor was it European, but it was a quiet place, especially at six-thirty in the morning, and its lack of commercial buildings—there were only a couple of bare, ugly apartment blocks as Dewey approached Packard—was soothing. At Packard, Dewey ended, and Emily jogged in place by a pizza restaurant while she waited for traffic. Then she crossed and continued east down a street called Wells.

She followed her usual route, moving on autopilot and trying to think through her reaction to the murder. She took a long, straight leg north, then a bend east and north again by a vintage apartment building with a convenience store on the first floor. This was her usual half-way point, but it offered little in the way of public space; today, she carried on. At Oakland, she turned back west and jogged through a block lined with small apartment buildings, running toward Arch Street and back toward Packard. On the other side, there was a half-block park, and Emily sometimes paused there to let her heart slow down and to do a few simple exercises. At this hour, it was usually empty, but this morning there was a young black man, also dressed for running, who was sitting on a bench. As Emily ran across between cars and into the park, slowing from a run to a walk, he got up and jogged slowly away down Arch and toward State Street. He passed her looking straight ahead, but Emily took note of him, partly because it was unusual to see anyone in the park and partly because he was memorable: obviously African, but with the bridge of the nose sharply defined, spreading to a broad and just slightly hooked shape. There was no excess weight visible, and the muscles of his arms and legs looked firm enough. Except that he was breathing heavily and not moving as a runner would, she'd have thought of him as one of the athletes with which the town was crawling. In the next second, she returned to her own concerns, and the young man was forgotten. After a few minutes of rest, she ran out onto Arch, west to State, and on back home. It wasn't much of a run, a bit over a mile, but Emily herself was no athlete, just a history graduate student trying to stay reasonably healthy.

When she walked up the steps to the front door, she drew in one last deep breath, and there it was, waiting for her like an overnight package: understanding. Her reaction to the death of Doctor Kirk wasn't grief, it was anger. Her plan was *entgleist:* derailed. Someone, some *Schweinebacke*, had thrown *einen Schraubenschlüssel* into the complex and delicate works of her life scheme. To throw a monkey wrench into something was not necessarily everyday German, but it had been part of an English class, one of a list of idioms to memorize, and now it came clearly to mind. Kirk had been part of a mechanism that she'd assembled, a machine that would grind slowly and in the end would produce Emily Weiden, PhD, a tenured, respected member of a faculty, preferably back in Germany, near her parents, back where people were considerate, polite, well-educated. She felt her eyes moistening again. The machine wasn't destroyed, but it had been damaged, damaged by some *Drecksau*. There was an almost physical straightening of her spine as she let herself into the apartment, a conscious hardening. Frustration and anger solidified into a tangible element in the mind of this young woman far from home.

... at the full ...

Belonwu Mbanugu was unusual for his generation. Although he was a capable and frequent user of the Internet, his enthusiasm for it was as a tool, not a toy. He watched as acquaintances played online games, and his reaction was boredom. There were no Orcs in reality, and he couldn't understand why anyone would spend time, let alone money, pretending to be one. Even the handful of Steampunk games that were out there held nothing for him. His fascination was with real Victorian objects and people and attitudes, not with digital representations of them. He liked owning nineteenth century technology or reproductions of it, since he could rarely afford genuine antiques. His self image was that of a craftsman, aspiring to become an engineer in the sense Rudyard Kipling would have meant that word. Some of Belonwu's favorite reading was the body of Kipling's stories about engineers, stories that set engineers on a pedestal, pieces such as *M'Andrew's Hymn* and *Bread Upon the Waters*. He knew by heart large parts of *The Ship That Found Herself*, and the acts of the engineer in *The Devil and the Deep Sea* were his equivalent of a treatise on ethics.

By the time he began applying to colleges, he knew without reservation that he wanted a degree in mechanical engineering or none at all. His high school grades in what passed for the hard sciences were outstanding, and he supplemented the rather pathetic classes and text books with his own research. His parents and especially his grandparents helped as much as they could, and even his sister managed to argue some small amount of cash out of her fiancé. But it was Belonwu's own efforts as much as anything that got him accepted at the University of Michigan. The day he knew the deal was done and that he was absolutely going to Ann Arbor was the high point of his young life.

When he moved, he left in the basement of his parents' house a modest workshop and a collection of strange old bits and pieces. He was fond of yard sales; his browser bookmarks included several local newspapers and their classified sections. Those sources and some email lists sent him back and forth on weekends, sometimes eastward into the suburbs, sometime west or north into the rural townships. He only bought things that were of real interest and only when he could get a real bargain; he enjoyed the hunt as much as the purchase and sometimes more than the ownership. There were things he wanted, things like an old brocade vest in reasonable condition (he was still looking for that item), and other things he'd buy on sight because they were old and interesting. His disposable income was limited, and the collection grew slowly. Once in a great while he'd sell or trade something, but it was rare.

In early April, Belonwu was at his parents' house in Gardner. His mother was upstairs, his father was out. He sat down in the only chair in his old workshop and cleared away tools and partly-built machinery from the top of the workbench. A hard object in his right hip pocket was uncomfortable, pressed against the unpadded seat of the chair, and he stood up and removed it. It was a small black powder derringer. He covered it with a cleaning cloth in case someone came in; his mother was seriously afraid of firearms. Now, with a workspace cleared, he opened his private notebook to a fresh page. He'd already looked through his collection of parts and gear and assemblies; he'd obtained some drawings from a text book and two more from sites on the Internet. He began to make a list of the things he'd need for his next project, a bill of materials with a column to indicate whether he already owned something or whether he'd need to get it.

"Cover; one; 45 sq feet; canvas—buy used sailcloth?"

"Lashings; 60 feet; leather laces?"

"Grommets; 5 x 2 per edge, x 8 edges = 80; buy 100"

"Linkages; multiple; brass rods - buy 6 feet"

"Plate; one; steel disk—use scrap piece"

"Pendulum, one; use old plumb bob"

"Supports, sides; four; use the sewing machine legs"

"Supports, internal; multiple; hammer formed—make from scrap"

"Bolts, cap nuts; brass; order on line"

"Revolvers, black powder replicas; four; buy @ gun show?"

... The Sea of Faith ...

It took Jerry Mbanugu a few years to build up a social shell around his actual, unmentionable history. The longer he lived and worked in the US, the more he could talk about that experience and avoid saying how and why he was here at all. Eventually, he began to have friends from his job, usually the other supervisors. Caught between management and the union, they had nobody to rely on except themselves, and since they were a small group, they tended to overlook race. To his white colleagues, Jerry was black, yes, but of a different kind than they were used to. He had a soft voice and a soft accent, quite at odds with his ability to lay down the law and kick asses that needed kicking. He was splendid at dealing with customers (most of them never saw him in person, and they thought of him as 'that English guy'). On his part, Jerry had no particular prejudices against anybody, always excepting people from the other side of the Nigerian conflict. The Hausa and Fulani he thought of as blood enemies, and he was wary of the Yoruba, since the Igbo believed they reneged on a promise to join the Biafran revolt. The African-Americans he met, though, were not first generation or anything like it, and they had no identification with African ethnicities. *Roots* was still a few years in the future; in the Detroit of the early seventies, there was plenty of black vs. white animosity, but little or no African vs. African.

Jerry had neighbors now, as well, and he gravitated toward a local church that several of them attended. By nothing more than chance, it was Episcopalian, and it took him almost a month to realize that the differences from the services he remembered were actually doctrinal, not just American. He had never been particularly religious, but by the same token, he'd never before set foot in anything other than a church of Rome. With a sense of guilt that surprised him, he bowed out politely and began seeking a Catholic congregation. He found one practically under his nose, right in Gardner. In his first confession as a returning sinner, he started off simply, explaining his long lapses. But the sheer relief of explaining himself to someone caught hold of him, and he told the priest the whole tale, from London to Nigeria to Detroit. When he finished, there was a short silence. Then, instead of severe censure and vast penance, he got three Hail Marys and a blessing. As Jerry left the confessional, Father Leo thought, *Absolutely barking mad, poor fellow*.

Jerry settled into an American routine. He went to work Monday through Friday, usually carrying a lunch. Sundays he went to church. That left Saturdays for shopping, working on his house, and perhaps doing something social. After a year in his congregation, those social events began to involve one particular young lady, Katherine, daughter of small businessman from Westland. Her family had no idea of their background, but she had a broad Igbo face and a wholly American sense of humor, and Jerry fell in love with her unreservedly. By then, if you ignored his somewhat sketchy car, he was an acceptable suitor, and she found him and his accent and his occasional naïveté about things American to be charming. They met at church events, then went to them together, and finally began to go on real, American-style dates.

There were differences between their ideas of male and female roles, but both of them were prepared to compromise; as things turned out, Jerry did most of the compromising. She was six years younger but with a lifetime in America and far, far more experience in the theory and practice of being a black woman in the rust belt. She'd read both Thoreau and James Herndon, and *The Way It Spozed To Be* resonated more with her than *Walden*. She told Jerry, in detail and without rancor, about 1967 in Detroit and about the Freedom Riders and the Klan. In turn, he told her about Biafra, and he was surprised that she knew some of it already, surprised to hear that aid for Biafra had been a brief cause in America. In the end, he told her almost all of it, without naming the Agency and without saying a word about diamonds left in the wall of a house. That was a secret he meant to keep.

Jerry and Katherine began to be a common pairing; people said, "Don't forget to invite Jerry and Katherine," and, "Ask Katherine and Jerry if they can help with that." To them, it was even more obvious. Neither of them ever put it this way, but it became clear that they were both refugees from something. Jerry had gotten away from Enugu and the civil war; Katherine's escape was less certain, the things she had to fear were still around. It was no surprise to anyone when they married.

In the first few years of the marriage, they had two children or rather one child, a boy, and a miscarriage. The experience of losing the baby and the risk for Katherine of another pregnancy brought an end to childbearing (and the Pope could like it or look the other way). Their son grew up with them in their Igbo-American household, and he found an actual Igbo bride, although she was unusual in being from a Jewish Igbo family. Neither of the two had followed their parents into religious practice, but the importance of relatives smoothed over the apostasy, by and large; having a family in America was simply going to be different than it would have been in Port Harcourt, and the grandparents adjusted. When the children could, they bought a house in Gardner, near Jerry and Katherine, and they also had children, a girl, Akunna, and a boy, Belonwu.

Those children knew their grandparents only as older people, people to be respected. Katherine was cheerful, loving, engaging; Jerry was a remote but friendly grandfather, and an unimpeachable source of lessons and guidance. He was also increasingly feeble. Jerry was already ill by the time Belonwu was in high school. He had trouble with breathing, an undiagnosed cough, and a shortness of breath. He blamed it on his years on the shop floor; Katherine, without any clinical reason, blamed it on his diet. Either way, he was retired and receiving disability payments from both an insurer and the government, and Katherine had also ended her career. Both were in their seventies, and it was unspoken but obvious that Jerry, at least, wouldn't live to see eighty.

On a rainy afternoon in March, Belonwu went to pay his usual visit to Jerry, now confined to his bedroom in the original Gardner house. He tended to go by himself, spanning the other family visits. The point wasn't to avoid his parents or his sister, just to add a visit, to make another event in the old man's slow days. Typically, he'd stay for an hour, less if Jerry seemed to be tiring, and they'd talk about his studies, the declining health of Belonwu's car, the right way to make shrimp and rice. Sometimes, Jerry would talk about things that happened on the job, when he'd been a machine shop manager. He'd draw lessons about handling people from his old experiences; he'd talk about quality and workmanship. Jerry approved thoroughly of the young man's career choice, and he appreciated the conversation about materials and manufacturing. His children and his granddaughter were constantly babbling about services and finance and digital this and that; this boy, on the other hand, was going to make things, he was going to be the honest, traditional engineer that Jerry had always tried to hire and never quite found.

Today, Belonwu found him in an unusual mood. After the opening pleasantries, Jerry's attention seemed to wander, as though he was only listening partially to Belonwu's story of an unfair and possibly inaccurate exam question. After a bit, the old man took over the conversation.

"My boy, will you bring me that letter ... there, on the desk?"

"Sure, *Ichie*. This one?" Belonwu had no real Igbo vocabulary, but he knew a few words of respect.

"Yes. Look at it, please, and tell me what you think I should do."

The letter was addressed to Jerry, written by someone Belonwu had never heard of, with a western name and a PhD after it. It asked if Jerry would be willing to provide information for a book about Nigeria, and it seemed to imply (*what!?*) that Jerry had some connection with the CIA.

"Grandfather, this guy is crazy, or he has the wrong address."

"This is hard for me," said Jerry. "I have been here, in the US, for so many years. I have never spoken to anyone about it. Sometimes I think that what I have said to people is the truth, but I always remember that it isn't."

Belonwu was confused, concerned. What was this letter doing to his grandfather? What wasn't the truth? The family story about Jerry's past was consistent and held in common. Everyone knew the same thing: he'd had a chance to escape the violence in Biafra, and he'd taken it, coming to America and then to Detroit. He'd worked for an aid agency, and they'd helped him and a few others get out and get citizenship. That was what Grandfather said, and beyond that, nothing else was ever said. It was implied that whatever family Jerry had had in Nigeria were victims of the war.

"This is for you only," Jerry said, slowly. "I have not been honest, but I could not be. I promised that I would say nothing. But I will not live long, now, and if they are willing to talk to this professor about me, I can talk about them."

"What do you mean, *them*, Grandfather?"

"Grandson, I will say this again: you must tell no one. When I was in Nigeria, after I came back from college in England, I worked for a company there, first in Port Harcourt, then in ... another city. That company was really gathering intelligence, keeping track of the war. They never said it, but it was the CIA."

"Seriously?" A foolish question; the old man was always serious. Belonwu had never heard him say anything that wasn't reasoned, well-considered, even sometimes pompous. Kidding was not in his makeup.

"I am serious. When the Government Army captured Enugu from us, and our leaders and soldiers had to go south to escape, I stayed behind. I pretended to be a refugee, and I reported on the enemy ... on the Government, you understand?"

"Yes. That's amazing, but yes, I understand."

The next few sentences came with difficulty. Jerry had rehearsed them many times, thinking of what he would say about himself and those days, if he were ever allowed to. It had been a long time, and he'd been ill, and the bare truth wasn't all that honorable, really. It didn't paint himself or the Agency in a very good palette. His life in Enugu, all but the last day of it, had actually been quite courageous, staying behind, defenseless, under the eyes of a racial and political enemy. But the important event, the thing he had to tell Belonwu, this boy who was the most responsible, well-behaved, respectful, and masculine member of his family, was not so flattering. He had, after all, run away. And so, the narrative as he told it was in some respects at odds with the facts.

"I was there in that city, Enugu, for a long time. But finally, there was an air raid and I knew they would round up all the Igbos, put us in camps or kill us. And so I asked to be taken out. Withdrawn, you see? And the CIA brought me here, gave me a passport and a place to live. And they said I must say nothing about them. But now they name me, and so I can speak of them, do you agree?"

Belonwu had no good answer for that. "Can't you check with them?"

"I have no one to call. The man who was my supervisor has retired, they said. And died since then."

"Are you worried about being in this man's book? Could you just say no?"

"I could. But I would like to talk about it. I would like people to know, finally, who I really was. And what I did. And I would like people to know what the Government did to Igbos, back then. Our war is forgotten. And now, Nigeria ... well, you read, you know what Nigeria has become. Your grandmother told me that even our great voice, Achebe, has passed on. It seems as though my talking about it might be the right thing."

Belonwu picked up the letter again, as he tried to think of a response. He glanced at it and realized with a start that the stationery said 'University of Michigan'.

"Grandfather, I think that if you want to talk to this guy, you should. I wouldn't care. Would Grandmother?"

"There's another thing to consider, though," said Jerry. "What do you know about Akunna and her husband?"

"Akunna? I ... I don't know. Are they having trouble?" Belonwu didn't see all that much of his sister since he'd gone off to school, and he saw even less of her husband. They'd only been married a few months.

"He is in trouble. He owes money to some people, more than he says he can pay. More money than I could loan to him. Akunna is unhappy because he is unhappy. And she thinks she is going to have a child. That would be wonderful, but not if there is no money."

"I didn't know that. I'm sorry. I wonder if there's anything I ..."

"No. No, the problem is larger than you could afford to think about. But the real trouble is that he owes the money to ... I will just say people on the side, if you understand. People who will not listen to reason or to excuses."

"I see. Charley's in trouble. I wish Akunna would have said something."

"He told her not to. He came to me himself."

That was a surprise. Charles Blake, the big shot car wash man, humbling himself to the in-laws; it was a hard scene to imagine, but gratifying. Even though Akunna's husband had kicked in a small amount for his education, Belonwu couldn't warm up to the man. He'd married Akunna, and so was clearly not averse to African-Americans, but he came across as a used car salesman, a small time white-guy businessman with no fresh ideas, a closet full of buy-one-get-one-free suits, and a Dodge Charger, the new version. If he'd at least gone to the effort to drive a *vintage* muscle car, Belonwu might have thought better of him. As it was, he fit into one of the young man's subconscious stereotypes. Although he'd almost forgotten the Fu Manchu novels, Belonwu still had a set of character templates left over from them, and Blake fit well into the pattern of the treacherous Anglo-Saxon renegades the Si-Fan was occasionally able to recruit. They were cheaply bought, never as efficient and deadly as their Asian or African counterparts, and completely expendable.

"Please don't speak of this," said Jerry. "But you need to know something else about Nigeria, something that if you can, you might be able to use to help Akunna." Belonwu noticed that he specifically said "help Akunna," not bringing Charley Blake into it.

"I cannot talk about how it happened," Jerry went on. "But when I was fleeing from Enugu, I was entrusted with something very valuable. It would have helped the Igbo cause, but I had to hide it. I couldn't take it with me." This was the version of events that Jerry had agreed upon with himself. He had never spoken the words, though, and they sounded especially false and self-serving as he said them. But he was committed, now, and the story would have to come out the way he'd scripted it.

"It was in a small envelope, and I was hiding in a house in the center of the city. When I thought they would find me, I put it into a hole in the wall, low down against the floor. I know where the house is, and I got your grandmother to show it to me on the computer a few months ago. I told her it was my mother's house. It was still there."

It took Belonwu a second to translate the last sentence; his grandmother was quite capable with the Internet and its offerings, and she must have been able to find the house for Jerry on some one of the satellite imagery sites. Operating the computer was not his strong suit, but he'd always been expert with maps, and once she found the city, the old man would have been able to point out the house he wanted with little trouble.

"What was in the envelope, Grandfather?"

Jerry's mind was in a trance-like state, not apparent to Belonwu or even to himself. Dazed with age and medications, the sheer impossibility of what he was about to suggest seemed to him as only a challenge to be overcome, a quest for this strong, young Igbo warrior to undertake and to win a king's ransom.

"Diamonds, Grandson. Many of them. If you can, go back to Nigeria, to the city of Enugu, and try to find them. They would solve Akunna's trouble and make the family wealthy. I will describe the room and the place I hid them. I leave them to you."

Belonwu couldn't meet the old man's eyes, and as he tried desperately to think, he glanced down at the letter he was still holding. It was signed by Allan G. Kirk, PhD.

... Sophocles long ago heard it ...

US Highway 12 cuts through Gardner from east to west. For reasons having to do with inexpensive land, questionable licensing deals, and the movements of sketchy people into and out of the area, there is a cluster of locally-owned motels. These places tend to be a few grades above the rock-bottom, but they're still affordably priced, and they have bland, generic names that can be changed quickly if necessary. Within one block on that spring morning, you'd find the San Francisco, the Red Knight, the Wayne Inn, the Northern, and the Congressional Motel. Andy and his colleagues had a suite—one bedroom, a bath, a sitting room, and a kitchenette—at the Congressional, their base for the Gardner corruption case. The location wasn't highly secure since it consisted of two long, straight buildings flanking an open parking lot. It backed up onto another parking lot, opening onto the next street south, and although there were curbs in the way, an SUV or even a boldly-driven car could get through and out the back. Or come in the back, for that matter. On the east side of the eastern block of rooms, though, there was only an industrial building, and only the bedrooms looked out onto it. As long as you weren't concerned about an armed assault, and if you were prepared to check periodically for listening devices and suspicious cars in the lot, it was an acceptable place for a clandestine meeting.

Today, dressed down for the occasion (they'd stopped blocks away and put their jackets and ties in the trunk of their Agency car), Andy and another agent, Mark Brenner, rolled in, parked next to a large van, and unlocked the first-floor room. The van hid their car from the casual observer on the street or sidewalk, and they spent as little time as they could getting into the room and out of view. There was no physical danger to themselves except possibly that of a random encounter with some kind of street druggie, but the confidential informant they were meeting would be worried, and reasonably so. He had quite serious personal problems, he said, and he wanted to offer information on the cheap tricks and fast plays that, he said, he'd encountered while trying to be an honest businessman in Gardner. He'd given them an obviously bogus name, 'Mavrides', but Andy and Mark already knew his real name and a great deal of his back story.

He was a US citizen, born in Warren to US citizens. He owned car washes here and there in the Detroit suburbs. His tax returns weren't all they really ought to be. He was married to a woman from Gardner. No children. He had credit problems of several kinds, and he'd been turned down recently for a business loan. Actually, he'd been turned down repeatedly. While they waited for him, the Feds flipped through the data they had.

"So his wife is from here?" asked Mark.

"Right. Married recently, I think? You got that profile there."

"Yeah, here it is. Wife's maiden name is ... what?" He passed the stapled report to Andy.

"Man ... no, Mbanugo. M-banugo. African-sounding. First name, Akunna."

"For a car wash guy, these were big loans he was trying for. Thirty-eight K, forty-two K. Does he think we're gonna pay him that kind of money?"

"I don't know what he thinks. He says he can give us people close to the mayor, maybe the mayor himself. He's into car washes. I guess he's got things to say about inspectors. That might get us to our pal, Jimmy Prine. Or if it's about parking or traffic tickets, well, that's this Ajax Gordon guy."

"Achilles Gordon," said Mark.

"Right, him. There sure are a lot of unusual names in this case."

"Whoops, here he is." Somebody knocked on the door. Mark dumped the reports into his briefcase and moved into the bathroom. Andy glanced through the peephole, then opened the door and stepped back. "Mr. Mavrides?" he said.

Charles Blake was slightly taller than Andy, wearing a generic dark suit, a white shirt, and a very dark blue tie. He had a chemically secured haircut, undisturbed by the breeze and styled to frame his high, flat forehead in a precise rectangle. His hair was dark although it had been darker earlier in his life, and there were touches of gray above his ears. He had no mustache, no beard; he looked less like a used car salesman, in fact, than he did like a small town mortician.

"Yes," he said, "I'm, um, Mavrides. Are you Agent Brenner or Agent Patel?"

"I'm Andy Patel. Hey, Mark." Brenner came out of the bathroom and set the briefcase down below the table. "This is Mark Brenner. Have a seat." Andy gestured to chairs in the slightly frayed front room. Both agents put their identification in plain sight. Blake took the hint and dug out a drivers' license and a business card. This put an end to the 'Mavrides' fiction, but it was kept in place, pro forma.

"We should make sure we're all on the same page," said Andy. "You know, obviously, since you called us about it, that we're looking into some issues here in the city."

"Yes, I know that," said Blake.

"Did you hear it publically or, ah, personally?"

"It was in the news. You interviewed the mayor, some of his managers."

"Okay," said Mark. "That's all?"

"Yes."

"You didn't talk with anyone or hear things informally about our investigation?"

"No, I don't really want anyone to know I'm interested."

"But you are," said Andy, "and you have information you think we should have?"

"I think I can help you, yes. I think there may be, you know, connections here that you may not have, uh, realized."

"Connections?" said Mark.

"Yes. That's all I really want to say until we, until you can ..."

"Until we ...?"

"Well, I have some problems, you know, some issues of my own."

Andy cleared his throat. "You need to understand that we have a very limited ability to offer financial compensation, Mr. Mavrides. There are other things we could talk about. Immunity, for example. Informal discussions with, say, creditors. But we don't really have the ..."

"I understand that," said Blake. "I'm, uh, really looking for help with some of the people who influence my business, you know. And, well, like you said, there are creditors."

Charlie Blake's situation was complicated. The car wash in Gardner had seemed like a bargain, and he'd cut corners on his due diligence. It was closed when he bought it, and having opened two similar shops before, he assumed that he knew what the procedure would be and roughly how much it would cost. His credit wasn't exactly sparkling, but he could pitch things well and in language bankers liked to hear. He got the funding for the purchase without too much trouble, and he got it from a normal, legitimate bank.

After he took possession, he made a list of the renovations and repairs that would be necessary, and he got the various interactions with the city under way. The cost of those things added up to a much larger number than he'd expected, and he had to go back to the bank and increase his line of credit. They were somewhat less enthusiastic this time, and the terms on the new money were more rigorous. Blake began to sweat a little.

The next problem came when the inspections actually started. One thing after another kept coming up, small issues with plumbing or electrical systems, mostly, and his initial efforts to comply with the city's strange and circuitous demands didn't seem to do much good. He'd fix one thing, and they'd find something else. Or they'd object to the way the fix was done. Months went by, the car wash stayed closed, and no money was coming in.

So Blake decided to raise a little hell. He went to the city's Engineering office and insisted on seeing a man named Jimmy Prine, the supervisor in charge of inspectors. Prine's opening position was to claim he'd never heard of the shop or Blake or any serious problems. He gave the impression that there were hundreds of retail facility inspections going on and the details of one of them wouldn't come to his attention. This was, of course, a flaming lie. Prine knew all about the car wash and had been waiting for its new owner to drop in. After Blake provided a few more sentences of explanation, Prine got the relevant files pulled and slowly flipped through them. When he'd kept Charlie sitting there for twenty minutes, he told him that the reports documented important non-compliances in the building and on the lot. He said that the inspectors had done a very good, very thorough job. He told Blake there was serious work to be done before he could expect to open.

If Charlie Blake had had a little more experience in dealing with civic officials in the older suburbs, he might have recognized the subtext in what Prine was telling him. But he didn't. Somehow, he'd managed to open two small businesses in the Detroit area without being shaken down, and he didn't understand what was happening now. He tried to walk through the inspector's comments one by one, disagreeing with them or denying that they were important. In each case, Prine politely referred him to local or state laws and regulations. When he ran out of patience with the one-by-one approach, Charlie make the mistake of asserting that neither of his two other locations had been subjected to this kind of scrutiny. At that, Prine became indignant, not with Charlie but with the poor quality of the inspectors in those other cities. He implied, very indirectly, that he might have to have a word with these people who were being so lax.

Up to this point, the game had gone very much as it always went. The businessman, who had no real leverage at all, would gradually retreat from each position, and as he fell back, Prine (or whichever city manager was doing the negotiating) would begin very delicately bringing dollars into it. It might start with an apparent concern over the investment that was at stake ("How much is it costing you not to be open?") An experienced entrepreneur would answer that with a ridiculously low value, and Prine would counter with another ("Oh, really? Only X dollars? I would have thought at least Y.") Eventually, there would be an agreement on a number and arrangements to make a payment—or several. But Charlie didn't understand the language. All he knew was that this petty official was standing in his way and causing him problems. He stormed out, making comments about his attorney. Prine was mildly surprised at this ploy, but he'd seen it before. He thought Charlie was playing the game. Prine's next move, as things usually went, would be to stick Charlie with another inspection and an even more expensive set of findings, bringing him back to the table in a more cooperative mood. Time was on the city's side.

And that might have been how it worked out; Blake could, in fact, have talked to his lawyer, and that gentleman would have explained what was going on. Charlie would still have been mad, but in the end, all might have been well. Unfortunately, when Blake stomped his way, furious at the city, Prine, and life in general, out of the building and back to his car, he found a parking ticket. He stared at it, then stared wildly up and down the street. No parking officer was in sight. No one was; it was not a street with a lot of foot traffic, and there was no target for his anger close at hand. He looked at the ticket again: expired meter, fifty dollars if paid within ten days. Blake went, as the saying goes, ballistic.

He turned around and stomped back inside. He waved the ticket at the woman whose job it was to direct extremely unhappy citizens to the right person. He demanded to know "what idiot" was in charge of the meter maids. The receptionist, not paid enough (in her opinion) to put up with this sort of thing, directed him to the office of Achilles Gordon.

It took a few minutes to get past the powerless individual in the outer part of the Traffic Department's small offices, but he did and he found himself, still enraged, in front of Gordon, sitting quietly on the other side of his desk. Things might still have gone well or at least gone better if this experience had been any different, but it wasn't in the slightest bit different than the talk he'd just had with Jimmy Prine. Gordon, calm and professional, took the citation from him and examined it. He asked if the car with that license plate was Blake's. He asked if it had been parked where the ticket said it had. He asked what, exactly, Mr. Blake thought was incorrect about the ticket.

What Blake thought was incorrect could not be explained simply or calmly. He yelled at Gordon for several minutes, making points about how he was here trying to do business with the city, how he was trying to open a car wash and create some jobs in Gardner, how, Goddamn it, he was being given the royal shaft by the city, the parking department, and every Goddamn body else. He wasn't going to put up with it any Goddamn more. This went on until he ran out of arguments, and a slight feeling of unease began to creep in. Blake was capable, after a period of time, of knowing when he was being out of line, and it occurred to him that complaining was one thing, but actually threatening people wasn't really the smartest tactic in a building full of public employees. He wound it down, and in an effort to save face, asked Gordon what he was going to do about it, 'it' being the ticket.

Achilles was not disturbed. Blake's tirade was the second one of the day and it would probably not be the last. Even better, unlike the first one, the cause wasn't the Department's fault. He'd need to check the database on the laptop, but he was already quite sure that this gentleman's name and license plate wouldn't be on it. No one had fouled up and ticketed someone who'd paid not to be ticketed.

He explained that he was personally sorry Mr. Blake had been inconvenienced, and that the reason was probably that there was no way for an ordinary parking officer to know who he was. The city did, indeed, value its businessmen and women, and there were measures in place to ensure that its officials knew who was who. That was not what Blake thought he'd hear. He just stared at Gordon.

"If you'd like, I can place you on our executive list," Gordon said. "The fees are quite reasonable ..."

"Fees? What are you talking about?"

"If we have your license plate number on record, Mr. Blake, we can ensure that you aren't ticketed or inconvenienced."

"Are you saying that if I pay you, you'll keep my car from being ticketed?"

"Or towed. Or stopped for minor traffic violations. Most businesspeople find it very convenient."

Suddenly, the day dawned. Charlie understood exactly what this bureaucrat was saying, but it took a few seconds to sink in. When it did, his mind instantly connected it with the conversation he'd just had with the Engineering department. He controlled himself with difficulty and clamped his jaw down on the things that occurred to him to say. Instead, he turned around and stalked out, leaving the ticket on Gordon's desk.

Charlie drove the few blocks to his non-functioning car wash, shut off the Charger, and sat staring out the windshield. It was a bleak view; nothing in sight was more than two stories tall; there were large open spaces between buildings, and the material of choice was concrete block. He could see a dry cleaners, optimistically painted bright yellow. There was an auto supply store, identified by one of those attractive signs from the sixties, where each letter of the words 'Auto Parts' was on its own fading plastic bubble, arranged vertically on a pole. Farther down the street, there was a competitor, another car wash; it had no visible customers at the moment, but at least it was open. Blake slammed his fist down on the steering wheel and reached for his phone.

He spoke briefly to a friend in Warren, and that person gave him another phone number to call. That number put him in touch with a gentleman who dealt in poorly-secured loans, loans that made up for their risk by the strikingly high interest rates they carried. He made an appointment to speak with the lender, tomorrow morning at a diner. Then he looked up the phone number for the Gardner mayor's office.

Blake wasn't all that impressive a man in person, and he was less so on the phone. Instead of getting Skootch Polowski on the line and reading him the riot act, he got first a secretary and then an assistant. The assistant listened to a disjointed narrative of corruption, coercion, and conspiracy, came to the conclusion that Blake was one of the many crazy people who were prone to calling up city government and complaining about things, and fobbed him off with a promise to take a message for the mayor. Once he got Blake off the line, he went back to surfing the web and forgot all about it.

Now as Kipling said, "Mark how things happen!" Perhaps Blake would have eventually settled with the city, gotten his car wash open, and adjusted his pricing upward to cover the increased costs. He might even have learned to ask a few more pointed questions before he leapt into a deal. The progress with getting the business running might have gotten him some slack from his bank and kept him from needing any further debt. But that is not what happened. Instead, he smacked the steering wheel again, drove home, told his new wife an edited version of the day, and had quite a bit to drink with dinner. The next morning, he was in no better a mood, worse, in fact, and he had to drive clear up to Waterford and meet the money man. He didn't get any return calls from the mayor. He did have a message from his formal banker, and he ignored that.

When he got tired of playing with his phone at stop lights, he turned on the radio. Detroit's big AM news station, WWJ, was babbling about the

Tigers, and Blake was about to hit the seek button when they switched to a local story, a story about Gardner. To Blake's astonishment, gratification, and glee, it appeared that Federal agencies were looking into rumors of corruption! It was said that they'd interviewed the mayor himself! If Blake had ever heard the term, he might have recognized the intense pleasure of *Schadenfreude*.

And that was the story, without the candor concerning his own business acumen, that Blake now told to two FBI agents, sitting across a coffee table in a cheap hotel.

"So that's it, then?" asked Mark Brenner. "You heard the Traffic guy ask for a fee, and you think the Engineering supervisor was doing the same thing?"

"Oh, no. There's more. Quite a bit more," said Blake.

"Good," said Andy. "Because we'd need more. All you've got there is Gordon, basically. And it's just your word on it. No offense, I believe it about that guy, but nothing ... there's nothing we could prove."

"Yes, I understand," said Blake. "There *is* more, for sure. And I think I can get a meeting with the mayor. On tape, I mean."

"So you'd be willing to wear a recording device?"

"Yeah, I would. You see, one of the things you should know is that I owe some money to a private lender. A guy up on the north side. He's kind of connected, has a Polish name." Andy and Mark exchanged a look; they knew about a guy with a Polish name, up in Macomb County.

"And when I mentioned that I was funding a business here, he said, 'Oh, yeah. You got Polowski down there as a mayor. I work with him'. He was really clear about that."

By mid-day, the conversation at the Congressional Motel had wound down. There was an agreement that Blake, still calling himself 'Mavrides', would set up at least an initial meeting with the Mayor of Gardner. Prior to that event, the Feds would give him a simple audio recording device—

100

the classic wire—and make sure he knew how to use it. On their part, if the results were promising they'd go have a conversation with Blake's loan shark, one that might result in a change in his business practices.

For a man with a date, Andy Patel wasn't as happy as he might have been. The meeting with Blake had been moderately disappointing; Blake didn't really know much, and he didn't seem like a man who could carry off a wired meeting without tipping his hand. If he could connect Gardner with a medium-sized loan shark, fine, but that guy wasn't Andy's case, and he'd have to hand the info off to those whose case it was.

His call with the CIA had been annoying. It meant he'd have to talk shop a bit with Jenn tonight, and although he'd enjoyed it before, he found himself resenting it now. He wanted to talk about folk music and food and what it was like to live in Ann Arbor. Gardner and most of the Detroit suburbs, for that matter, depressed him. Urban sprawl is ugly when it's new, when the plastic signs are at least shiny and the pavement is smooth. Old sprawl is repellant, empty, unwanted, a reminder on a vast scale of the throw-away culture. From coffee cups to whole cities, we use it up and pitch it and move on to something else. This train of thought led to a kind of simple guilt, too. He'd gone through a few plastic water bottles in his time, and he honestly didn't know how to clean up a kitchen without using paper towels. On top of that, he lived in one of these older suburbs himself, in a condo, on a street that could use some repaving. It wasn't all that different from where he'd lived outside Cleveland. A thought slipped around the edge of his consciousness as he drove back to the office, a thought that maybe the salary of two cops, added together, might cover a reasonable place in a real town and still buy the gas for a commute into Detroit.

... the moon-blanched land ...

June first, 2013. The date stood out on Belonwu's calendar, marked with a day-long event. It said only 'D' in bold white text on a red background. It wasn't an unbreakable cipher; it simply meant 'decide'. It was the date on which he'd decided he had to decide what to do. He'd made preparations of several kinds, but he'd taken no action that couldn't be cancelled, revoked, or abandoned. Yet. Very shortly, though, he would have to commit, and once committed, his options would narrow dramatically. Today, he was nothing more than a U of M undergraduate, with a relatively good GPA and very little else. Within a week, if he decided to do what his plan called for him to do, he might be something quite different. His life would change; there was no question about that.

All of it, all of the carefully planned steps, stemmed from two conversations with his grandfather. The first one had stunned him with its wild improbability. How could he fly off to Nigeria, find a house in an obscure city, and remove a parcel of diamonds from a hole in its wall? The old man had met each objection with a solution: he would pay for the travel; Belonwu already had a passport; he could get a visa easily enough, as a tourist; the house would be easy to find: it was on both satellite images and maps of the town; he would draw a diagram of the house itself, showing where the diamonds were; Belonwu would buy a hammer or a pick locally; he would enter the house when there was no one about. It all seemed logical and clear and feasible, especially to Jerry Mbanugo. To Belonwu, it seemed insane. *Was* his grandfather insane? Or was this nothing to a man who'd fought in a tragic war, deceived the enemy, escaped and remade himself into an American? And above all, how could he refuse?

And so, on the basis of that first discussion, he began at least to plan the steps. Then, he went back again for another visit to the old man's bedroom, and he found that the sand had shifted. Jerry gave him the sketch of the house, a treasure map essentially, with an X marking the hiding place. He appeared to be as sound of mind as before. Then, blandly and without making it seem important, he pulled the rug out.

"That is the map I drew for you and for Doctor Kirk," Jerry said.

"For who?"

"That Doctor Kirk who wrote to me. We had a long conversation. I told him all about my work there, and all about the suffering of the people. I told him how I was chased through the streets by a mob, how I hid in that house, how I put the diamonds into the wall. I told him that an Igbo warrior was going back to get them."

"You told that Professor?" Belonwu was stunned. "You told him I was going to Enugu?"

"Oh, no, my boy. I did not tell him *who* was going. That must be a secret. Just between the two of us."

"And you gave him this map?"

"Oh, yes. I don't think he believed me, at first, and so I gave him this ... a copy of it, you understand ... to prove that I was remembering it all as it happened."

"But he's writing a book! Everybody'll know!"

"His book will take a year or more for him to write. You'll be back long before then. I'll be gone ... yes, it's true, I don't have much time now. Your name will not appear. Only you and he will know what was done, and only you will know it was you. You see, I've thought it all through."

Chineke! thought Belonwu. *At least I can swear a bit in Igbo*.

He was torn, then and for days after. On one side of the fight there was America, college, courses to be passed, a graduate program to be found, an assignment to be turned in yet this term. On the other, there was a mystic appeal. He was being chosen for a quest, an adventure, danger and reward, honor to be won and sacrifice to be made. It would be for the good of the family; perhaps if the pot of gold were big enough, something could be done for poor old Nigeria, too. For the Igbo people, for his ancestors in the name of his grandfather, the bold. Belonwu never had a chance, really. It was too much like his childhood games, too much like hearing the call of the Si-Fan.

And so he'd worked it all out. There were multiple levels of security to deal with. The trip itself had to be kept closely held; it couldn't be kept secret, since there were people who'd know he was gone, official records of his travel and the purchase of tickets, missed classes to account for, but it could be minimized, described to the family as Grandfather's last request, sending Belonwu back to the old country for pictures and, perhaps, to see if there were any relatives still living. Under that guise, then, it followed that it had to be done quickly, since the old man was clearly dying.

Next, there was the recovery of the diamonds. That would be something between Jerry and Belonwu alone. Until he was back in the US and the gems, in the extremely unlikely case that he actually got his hands on them, in some kind of safe storage, nothing must be said about them. He'd done his best to impress Jerry with that: "I won't be safe over there if anyone else knows what I'm trying to do."

The third level was something for himself alone. No one must know that he'd taken his plan down another avenue, done another analysis of the situation, and concluded that Allan Kirk was a risk that could not be accepted. He hated the thought, hated the probability tree he'd drawn (and quickly destroyed), hated the fact that he already knew the outcome before he'd done the arithmetic. If anyone knew what Belonwu was up to, his chances of getting out of Nigeria, diamonds or no diamonds, were poor to none. Doctor Kirk could not live to write his book or even to discuss it.

Belonwu pointed his cursor at June sixth and created a new calendar entry; 'E' for 'execute'.

... and then again begin ...

On Friday morning, the fourteenth of June, sunlight was coming in Jenn Langton's bedroom window. She owned a small house on the far west side of town, and it was oriented in the same way as Allan Kirk's: facing west with the bedroom at the rear, situated to get morning sun. As she sat up, the alarm went off, and that prompted a quick review. She rubbed her eyes. It was Friday, a work day, she had to get up, shower, eat something, and get into the office. "Into the office! Christ!" She remembered the CIA and then the rest of the evening.

She'd started to tell Andy, almost as soon as he came in the door, about the case, about what they knew and the vast amount they still didn't. But the look on his face stopped her. He'd told her, quickly and in a kind of formal, briefing voice, about the call from Divina San Martin. About how he'd said he'd speak to his 'contacts' in Ann Arbor, how he hadn't given any names. That he'd call San Martin back or Jenn could, but sooner or later, she'd probably have to talk to the spooks.

It took the wind out of her sails. She'd seen this agency-professional aspect of Andy's persona before, but only in a room full of his superior officers. To have him use it with her, especially in the first five minutes of a date, threw her off her social game. Worse, his assumption that she'd be reluctant to call someone in the CIA hit her hard. She knew that the first time she'd had to cooperate with a federal agency, she'd screwed it up. That had been the FBI, three years ago, before Andy was even in Detroit, and she thought it was history. Apparently not. Apparently someone had said, "Langton isn't all that good at working outside her organization."

The reality was: *no*, no one had said that. No Fed other than Andy knew she was involved with the Kirk case, and Andy didn't know anything about her earlier problems. He was behaving as most government people behaved when it was necessary to cross territorial lines, playing it close to the chest. To him, it would have been a gross indiscretion to tell San Martin, "Yeah, I know those cops. Call this Langton person, it's her case." That he was candid with Jenn about the call was a mark of his respect for her; with someone he didn't know, he'd have been just as round-about as San Martin had been with him. He had no sense that, to Jenn, he sounded cold and slightly patronizing.

"I see," she said. "Did you think I ..." Her whole expression had changed, and Andy was caught off balance. "Why wouldn't I want to call her?"

"Um, I don't get that," Andy said. "You will have to call, I imagine. Or she'll call you, once I make the contact."

"Oh, I'll call her. Give me the number."

"Sure, I've got it ... somewhere here. Here it is." He gave her the note from his boss.

There was a short pause; Jenn put the information in her purse. "Do you know what they want to know?" The coolness was still there in her voice.

"Yeah." A pause. "Jenn, are you ... Did I step wrong, here?" He had a thought, suddenly. "Is your department trying to keep the case, ah, quiet? Should I have played dumb?" He couldn't imagine how he'd have played any dumber than he had, but if this was political ...

"No," she said. "It's nothing. I just wonder why you thought I wouldn't want to talk to the Feds."

"I didn't. I just told this person I'd get back to her with a contact. Just to get her off the phone."

"Really?" Some of the edge came off her tone. "I thought ... I just thought there might be some concern. Concern about me."

Andy was baffled. His image of Jenn, professionally, was that of a smart, effective city cop. He'd been on that one case with her and MacArthur, last year, and although the case as a whole was a fiasco, she'd done good stuff, searching a barn where one of the many suspects had stashed drug-contaminated money. Whatever problems there'd been hadn't been hers.

"I don't know what you're getting at. As far as I know, I'm the only one in the office who even knows you."

"Markowitz didn't say anything about me?" Doug Markowitz was an agent, now retired, who'd worked with Ann Arbor frequently. He'd had to straighten out the various levels of ruffled feathers Jenn had caused.

"No, not that I recall. He introduced you, I remember that." *And I owe him for that*, Andy thought.

Jenn relaxed, at least partly. "I'm sorry. Forget it. Long day. I misunderstood what you were trying to tell me."

Whatever she'd been thinking of, Andy decided instantly that it was not in his best interest to know. Not now, anyway. They both stepped carefully around the shop talk for the next few minutes, allowing the chill to dissipate. Then, as they went out the door, Jenn slapped her forehead.

"Duh!"

"What?"

"I forgot. We were kidding around about the CIA just this morning! We found letters between them and Kirk. Him asking for information, them saying yes or no."

"Wow!" Andy was trying hard to be pleasant, charming, enthusiastic, and boyish, almost to the point of pathos. "So you knew about it already?"

"I told MacArthur it wouldn't be the top thing on my list. Wrong again, Langton." Her laugh carried down the block.

Jenn drove, and they parked in a lot on Ann Street. They walked up Main, past a towering example of the ziggurat building style affected by a particular local architect, went across Huron, and entered the city's adult (as opposed to 'student') restaurant district. They turned down Washington and got a table outside at the old Earle. Except for a bank at the corner and an ancient locksmith's shop, the whole block was given over to dining. The Earle itself was in a basement, but their handful of sidewalk tables offered the same menu and the same wine list, and it gave you what passed in Ann Arbor for a view, out west across the valley of the hidden Allen Creek and into a pale sunset.

"This is sort of the edge of town, true?" Andy asked.

"Well, the edge of downtown. The city goes out past where my house is."

"It's nice. I like this kind of block. It feels ... it's filled in. I mean, there aren't those big gaps for parking." He was looking east along Washington. Jenn smiled slightly, since directly behind him was quite a large parking lot. It was rare, though, she admitted. Most of the gaps in downtown were used or about to be used.

"I've been here almost, I think ... twelve years," she said. "I like it. I like it better than anyplace else I've lived, at least."

"Do people live downtown? Are there apartments or condos?"

"Not as many as the city'd like, I guess," Jenn said. "But yeah, there are places. Parking is an issue, though. And traffic."

"I suppose. You'd have to work something out. Expensive, too, right?"

"That I don't know. I didn't look down here when I was buying. I just assumed I couldn't afford it."

"Oh, well. So ... wine?"

They ate and went to their concert. The Ark, a venerable folk club, was hosting a Celtic band from Detroit, fiddles and a dulcimer and the *bodhran*. It was lively music and sad, too, hard to hear without the reminder of mortality. The people who first played it and heard it and danced to it went home early and got up before dawn for another day of hard work for small return in a short life. A pair of rank-and-file cops in twenty-first century America could feel almost cosseted by comparison. The walk back to Jenn's car was quiet and thoughtful.

And now, come Friday morning, there wasn't another head on Jenn's pillow or another car in her driveway. But she discovered, coming out of the shower, that she wished there had been. Andy'd reached out for a handshake, and it had become more of a hand clasp, but then he'd gone home, practicing his mother's old policy, not being a jerk.

... The tide is full ...

Tactics in a modern urban setting are not taught in high schools or undergraduate classes, at least not in an engineering curriculum. If you're intent on enforcing the law or suppressing revolt, you'd find it a lengthy and complicated study. If you're on the other side of the desk, focused on circumventing the forces of law and order, there's a bit less to learn. Except in the most extreme cases (outright, formal revolution, for example), you'll have the initiative, the opportunity to select when and where to act. And the specific skills you'll need are mostly in the realm of escape and evasion: in civilian terms, 'sneaking'.

Sneaking around a populated, developed area is not really a matter of camouflage in the traditional sense of the word. There's not much point in looking like a tree or like desert sand if those things aren't part of the scene. Instead, you want to look like something ordinary that *is* there, something that belongs there, something that won't attract attention. In an American subdivision, the choices are limited, especially if you're going to be carrying a large package. Under those circumstances, you should strongly consider looking like a deliveryman.

Belonwu didn't take this approach to its extreme, mostly because he didn't have the time or money to set himself up as the fullest, most realistic simulation of a man from Federal Express or UPS. Instead, he bought brown slacks and a matching work shirt from a uniform store, replaced his usual boots with his one pair of dress shoes, and covered his hair with a dark-colored ball cap. There was nothing he could do about his car. It was a faded blue Toyota sedan, and no one would ever mistake it for a delivery truck. That was just a risk he had to take, and he planned on minimizing it.

Looking at Professor Kirk's house and neighborhood with on-line maps, he noted that the lot backed up onto a small park, and he'd allowed himself one drive-by to confirm that the park along with the blocks surrounding it would be largely deserted at two-thirty in the afternoon. His plan was to start with the park and, if it was empty, approach the house that way. If not, he'd keep right on going, park in Kirk's driveway as a deliveryman would, and work as quickly as possible. And if Kirk happened to be home, well, that would be just too bad. He had an idea for avoiding that risk, though.

It was Thursday, June sixth. At one-thirty, Belonwu drove down Kirk's street, slowly, looking right and left as though he was trying to find an address. When he passed the house of interest, he noted that there was no car in the driveway. He was able to confirm what he'd seen from the online system's street view: the garage door had a handle, meaning that it was probably manual, not powered. He kept on going, seeing no one in the yards or on the sidewalks. His car was nondescript, and he'd used black tape to turn a '9' on his license plate into an '8'. It wouldn't fool a cop for a minute, but if a civilian remembered seeing a blue 1991 Camry, the altered number wouldn't come back to the right car, and the police would question the accuracy of the rest of the description.

He drove to the end of Playwright Lane, turned left to leave the subdivision, and then went north on Green Road. He turned off into a hotel parking lot, stopped, and took out his phone. He dialed Kirk's home number, and no one answered. Then he called Kirk's office.

"This is Allan Kirk."

"Yes, Doctor Kirk?"

"Yes, speaking. What can I do for you?"

"This is Fred, from Publisher's Delivery. Sir, were you expecting a delivery today?"

"No. I'm not expecting anything ... or, wait. Is it a package or an envelope?"

"Just a minute, sir." Belonwu paused thirty seconds. "Sorry for the wait, sir. Yes, it's an envelope. But I'm calling to say that unfortunately it won't be there today. So if you were waiting for us at ... " again, he paused, and then he pretended to read off the address, "We won't be there until tomorrow."

"All right," said Kirk. "I don't know what it is, anyway. And I won't be at that address tomorrow, either. Not during the day. Do you need a signature?"

"Not if you authorize us to leave it. Is that acceptable, sir?"

"Yes, that's fine. Couldn't be important, anyway."

"Thank you, sir. Have a good day."

So Kirk was not at home, and he wouldn't be at home for the afternoon. In one way, Belonwu was pleased; in another, more visceral way, he wasn't. Instinctively, he wanted a reason to cancel the mission. Like a patient who hopes his dental surgery will be postponed, he knew intellectually that what he planned to do was essential, but he still shrank from it.

It was now closing in on two o'clock, and he moved from his obscure spot behind one hotel, through connecting parking lots to a place behind a second one. He sat there, pretending to make calls or read mail on his phone, for another fifteen minutes. Then he put on a pair of latex gloves and headed back out to Green Road.

The park behind Kirk's house wasn't one of the city's most landscaped. In fact, it was almost treeless, and it offered little in the way of concealment or cover. It was small, though, only the width of three lots and as deep as one, and as predicted, it was empty. He parked and moved quickly, opening the left rear door and pulling out the device. He'd considered covering it but decided it would be pointless. If he was stopped by the police, a blanket over the thing would just look more suspicious, and if someone saw him carrying it, a covering would make it seem odder and more memorable. There'd be only a few minutes of exposure, walking through the park with it. And of course, walking back with it later; he pushed that thought away.

Belonwu pulled his cap down and carried the device across the park, carefully not looking around, trying to seem as though he knew what he was doing. It took less than a minute to reach the hedge that defined the west side and, as he'd hoped, people and dogs had made a gap into the Kirk backyard. There was no fence; the wire cutters in his back pocket wouldn't be needed. He walked up to the back of the garage and set the device down beside the door.

The lock was trivial, cheaply made. It was hardware store merchandise, and in fact, it wasn't locked. The owners had lost the keys and never bothered to do anything about it, nor had Kirk. Belonwu didn't know that, though. He looked at it closely, took out a simple table knife, and slid the blade into the gap. He applied a small amount of leverage, and the catch moved back. He didn't notice that it would have opened on its own. He opened the door as quietly as he could and looked around; the garage was nearly empty, and there was a substantial amount of dust on the floor. He took a pair of polypropylene clean room booties from a pocket (he'd appropriated them from one of the school's labs), and pulled them on over his shoes. Then he picked the device back up and carried it carefully inside. He set it down where he considered it would be most in the way, where it would have to be moved before a car could come in. He knew that Kirk used the garage because it was largely empty and because of the tire marks in the dust.

Belonwu knelt down beside the device and peered at the supports—the feet—it rested on. He noted the marks he'd made on them, only on one side. It let him know that he was on the correct side for unlocking the mechanism. He slipped his left hand, palm upwards, under the covering and near a corner, where the lowest piece of wrought iron in a sewing machine leg arched up enough to make room. There was a loop of brass rod, big enough for a finger, and he gently pulled it back toward himself, extracting the whole piece. He stood up and slipped the rod down the outside of one pant leg, hooking the loop over his waistband. He went back out the door, took off the booties, and moved cautiously around the side of the garage, toward the front.

There was just room between the building and the hedge for him to move. When he got to the end of the wall, he looked carefully out and then up and down the street. No one was visible. He took a deep breath and walked around the corner to the middle of the garage door. Willing himself to think like a tradesman, to act like a tradesman, to *be* a simple, honest repair guy, there to do something to an old door, he knelt down again. His back was to the street; he reached into a shirt pocket and fished out a very small tube of superglue, the thick, gap-filling kind. He injected most of the tube's contents into the keyhole. Then he got up and, still holding the tube in his gloved hand, walked around to the back yard again.

He closed the back door but made sure it was unlocked. He noted the state of house lights: garage lights, off; kitchen lights (visible through a door wall), off. Without going around peeking in windows, that was all he could determine, but it would be enough. He took his gloves off and put the super glue tube well down into one of the fingers, the table knife into another. He stuffed that glove into the other one and put all of it back in a trousers pocket. He looked through the gap in the hedge and saw nothing but an empty playground and his car, parked where he'd left it. In another minute, he was driving away. Now the worst part began; now he'd have to wait.

... upon the straits ...

At ten o'clock on Friday morning, Jenn's phone buzzed and played a few notes of Bill Frisell's version of *Shenandoah*; it was her calendar alarm sound. She'd set a recurring event for that time, and the title was simply 'Call Mac'. The significance of needing a reminder for it didn't occur to her; she just felt bad about forgetting to keep him updated.

"MacArthur ... hi, Jenn."

"Hi, Mac. Can you talk right now?"

"Sure. I'm at the hospital, anyway. Just the usual, visiting my pals the oncologists."

"But just routine, right?" she asked. "I mean, nothing new?"

"No, no. I feel fairly good, to tell the truth. I come to see these guys once a month, and we argue about how much of which drugs I should be taking when. It's fun."

A lot of this was untrue. He felt pretty damned bad, in fact, certainly compared to how he'd felt when he was fifty. Keeping up with the changes in medication was annoying, even for a structured thinker, used to following complex instructions. He wondered how in the hell the elderly and confused managed to take the right doses. (That he wasn't among the elderly and confused himself, he took for granted. Others might have disagreed.) And seeing the oncology team wasn't much fun; since he wasn't actually dying on them, they regarded him as a success. They were growing tired of his complaints about bone and joint pain, lack of energy, sinus problems, random itchiness. Hidden behind their professional mien was the suggestion that, "You know, it could be a lot worse." It was true, though, that he wasn't suffering from anything new, and he'd long ago internalized the idea that in most cases of cancer, no news was good news.

He was in a waiting room on floor seven of the university's newest hospital building. Reception wasn't great, and he got up and moved to the window. The view from this high up was always interesting, since Ann

Arbor had only recently stopped discouraging tall development. In a decade, there'd be more high points around town, but today, a seven-story prospect (or six or eight; the U of M health system had a strange reluctance to just start numbering floors at one and go up from there) was still a bit of a treat and worth savoring.

"So," Jenn said, "I wanted to give you the latest. It's curiouser and curiouser."

"Oh, good. I hate it when somebody just shows up and confesses. Takes all the mystery out of life."

"Not much hope of that, so far. First, you know how we were talking about the CIA yesterday? Because Kirk had some correspondence with them?"

"Sure."

"Well, I got a call from ... I saw Andy last night." No reason not to let Mac know, but it seemed a little like revealing a confidence. "And it turns out, his office got a call from the CIA! About Kirk!"

"No! Why?"

"I have to fill in a few gaps, because the woman I talked to ... Andy gave me the phone number. He doesn't want to be in the middle. Or at least he didn't. Maybe he will now."

"Why?"

"Hold on. This only makes sense in sequence. So, I called this woman in Virginia, somewhere, and it turns out she's in a department that you get shunted to if you want access to old documents. And her area is West Africa, Nigeria, like that. So she knew Kirk's name."

"All right."

"And she saw a news story about him being murdered. She didn't tell me all that much, voluntarily, but I did get her to say, finally, that they just really want to know where we are with the case, and if we have suspects, and so on. I'm reading between the lines, but I think they're worried about any kind of PR, you know, good, bad, or indifferent."

"Not all that surprising, I suppose," said Mac. "Think about how hard it is to get the FBI to tell you anything." He was concentrating on Jenn's narrative, and the irony of that last statement escaped him. Jenn hadn't had any trouble getting the FBI to talk to her, but he missed the implication.

Jenn didn't. She laughed and said, "Oh, they're going to talk to us, all right. Wait until you hear all of it."

"Okay."

"So when she mentioned 'suspects', I took the opportunity to try to pry things out of her, like, for example, who Kirk was researching. Names, that is. And she tried to put me off ... I don't think she really knew without looking up the requests ... but she finally came across with three, one western name and two Africans."

"Anybody we'd heard of already?"

"That's the next part. So I called Andy, just to let him know that I'd touched base with the CIA, and ... well, you know, he's interested because he was there when we found the device. So I told him the names. Guess what?"

"He knew them?"

"One of them is the maiden name of somebody's wife, somebody he knows about, I mean."

"Somebody here?"

"In Gardner. You can't tell anybody that, by the way. Nobody's supposed to know there's a case going on. But there is, looking at city officials or something, corruption."

"It's not *very* secret. Hell, it was in the news a while back."

"Oh. Well, that was probably just Andy being a Fed, then." Jenn was momentarily annoyed that she hadn't seen the story, but she let it go. MacArthur was retired, after all. He had time to read the news.

"So where are you going to go with it?" Mac asked.

"It gets better. I did some quick checking. There's a family with the name. Mbanugo. In Gardner. The specific guy Kirk was interested in was Jerry Mbanugo, but it turns out he's dying of something. He's been at home in bed for months. He's got a wife and a son and a daughter-in-law ... have to check on them, but they seem to be unlikely for us, I mean as suspects. The son went to college, but it was Wayne State, not U of M. But here's the interesting part: there's two grandchildren, one of them is married to somebody in Andy's case and the other one ... is a U of M engineering student right here in town!"

"Son of a gun," said Mac. He was impressed, both with Jenn's having gotten all that data together in the course of a morning and with the complexity of the threads, the baffling links among people that sometimes turned up. This murder could still be a simple jilted-girlfriend thing or a drug thing or a robbery thing, but now it had a whole new complexion. "Do we know anything about the kid?"

"Not enough yet. That's why I called you, actually." That was only partly true. Jenn didn't want Mac to feel left out, especially left out of this case since he'd been there for the first act, in his neighborhood, in front of his friends' house. She knew already what she planned to do next, but she owed it to Mac, it seemed to her, to get his opinion, too. "Are you going to be done over there at the hospital in time for lunch?"

"Uh, let's see. What time is it? Ten-fifteen? Yeah, sure. I'm just waiting for them to cut me a new prescription for something, and then I'm out of here. Where do you want to go?"

"I'm downtown now, and I'll go up to the scene after lunch, so: Northside, again?"

"Been to Angelo's lately?" Mac countered.

"Angelo's! Not in a long time. Great. Eleven-thirty?"

"I'll be there."

"Oh, hold on. I meant to say, the bullet in Kirk? It was from one of the guns in the device. No doubt, the device shot him."

MacArthur wasn't fond of phone calls. Generally, they were an interruption of something else, usually longer than they needed to be, and frequently imprecise. That last one, though, was a real exception. It was full of information of many kinds. For one thing, it seemed to show that Jenn still wanted his help or at least his observational ability (and he remembered, smiling, that at a crime scene full of cops and detectives running around, *he* was the one who found the missing bullet. *And* the glued-shut garage door lock. Bunch o' young whippersnappers).

Even more interestingly, now they had a name, somebody with a connection to Kirk—a tenuous one, but still. Those links would take some thought, maybe even a diagram. Somewhere in there, it felt as though there'd be a smoking gun or an unimpeachable alibi or something. Very unlikely, he thought, to be a complete coincidence.

And of course, Andy and Jenn. So she 'saw' Andy last night, eh? That wouldn't have been a coincidence, either. What was it she'd said? "Just Andy being a Fed." That sounded like a fairly personal comment. Well, good. Very good. He wondered if there was anything he could do to foster things; he decided against it. Wait until a need arises.

Mac took out a small notebook and sketched a diagram. He drew bubbles labeled 'Kirk' and 'CIA', and connected them with an arrow. He drew another one, 'UM', and linked Kirk to that. And UM linked to 'Mbanugo Grandson'.

He drew an arrow from CIA to a new bubble, 'FBI', and one from there to 'Gardner'. He added a link from FBI to 'AAPD'. Then he put in a final entity, 'Mbanugo Grandfather', and pointed the CIA at that. What was missing, unfortunately, was an arrow from AAPD to anyone, grandfather or grandson or anybody else. He stared at the picture; it didn't answer any questions, yet. But if there was anything to be learned, at least about

Jenn's case, it would be along that path from Kirk, through the university, and to the grandson. They needed to be much more familiar with that young man. Much more.

While Mac was drawing and pondering, Jenn made another call. She got Emily Weiden's voice mail (Emily scrupulously turned off her phone in class). "Emily," she said, "This is Detective Langton. We talked earlier in the week. About Professor Kirk. I wonder if you could come to my office on Monday? I hope I'll have some pictures to show you by then, people I want to see if you know. Can you call me?" She left her number.

Emily. Emily was a piece of it all, maybe. She'd been at Kirk's place, at least after he was killed. That was certain. And she said she'd been there once before, at a party. Probably true; why would she lie about that? But what else was there? Why was she the only one of Kirk's students who worried about his being gone? There were at least three others working with him; didn't they need him around for something? Larry Whitaker had talked to two of them, at least on the phone, but that wasn't all Larry did on the phone; he was phoning it in, these days, doing as little as he could, staying out of trouble, hanging on until retirement. That was Jenn's assessment, anyway. Whatever conclusion he came to about the grad students, Jenn would check it herself.

Emily. Now, with the CIA thing going on, Jenn had another thought about Emily. She was a non-citizen. A foreign national, from Düsseldorf. Could that possibly mean anything? Somebody in the department was checking Emily's status, her visa and so on, but not as a priority, and certainly not in any detailed way. Emily had said that her thesis was about right-wing groups; Jenn remembered vaguely that some right-wing stuff was actually illegal where Emily came from. Would that make it harder or easier for her to do historical work on the subject? MacArthur had known from memory the name or at least the acronym of a French security agency; Jenn wondered if he knew anything about Germany.

... neither joy, nor love, nor light ...

As Thursday night crept along, Belonwu visited a series of public places: a couple of cafes, a sub shop, the Graduate Library. These were all places he'd been before, and he looked closely at the people who spoke with him, remembering faces, memorizing names from ID badges or the server name on receipts. These would be the people who, with luck, would remember him and be able to confirm his presence in their establishment, on a given evening and within a range of hours. He'd changed into his usual clothes, leaving the slacks and work shirt in the car and the car in his apartment parking space. Now he was dressed in his usual slightly Victorian affect, partly because that was how he normally dressed and partly because it would be easy for people to remember. He didn't like drinking all that much, and he objected to the noise of the campus-area bars, so he didn't bother with the taverns along State Street. Instead, he spent the bulk of the evening in an espresso shop, nursing a few cups of coffee and running over outcomes in his mind.

He had an intelligence gathering problem. For the task of planting the device, he'd been able to confirm, with an acceptable degree of certainty, that Kirk wasn't home and that, probably, no one else was. There had been a few unknown elements, but the key requirement, private access to the house and the garage, had been fairly easy to guarantee.

Now, though, the situation was much more complex. His next steps would be ruled by a whole range of possible outcomes. He was scrupulously not writing things down or listing them on his phone, but he sorted them out in his mind: *one*, the device worked, Kirk was hit and died, and nobody noticed. *Two*, just like one, but somebody heard or saw something, and the police had been called. *Three*, Kirk was only wounded, and again, the cops are involved. *Four*, Kirk or someone else finds the device, but doesn't set it off (or it malfunctions); the cops are involved. *Five*, for some reason, Kirk doesn't find it, doesn't set it off, ignores it, isn't concerned; it's just sitting there, still armed, waiting for someone to mess with it. If he'd been an electrical engineer, he might have built a device with communication capabilities, at least to the point of sending a text message when it went off. As a mechanical engineer and a somewhat lapsed Steampunk, he'd created a machine without electronics, and he was going to have to rely on humint—human intelligence—to find out what had gone down.

Although he hadn't recognized or objected to the modernity of it, part of his plan did benefit from a communications intelligence capability. His smart phone had an application that could monitor emergency services radio, and it was running now as he sipped coffee and pretended to read a text book. His earphones played an intermittent series of static-punctuated calls between Ann Arbor and Washtenaw County law enforcement personnel. So far, nobody was talking about anything exciting at all. It was too early in the evening for drunk and disorderly complaints and long enough after rush hour for traffic to have settled down. Out in one of the townships, there was a domestic disturbance issue being worked; otherwise, not a lot else was going on. He'd keep the scanner on and the ear phones in for the duration.

To cover the simple case of Kirk being home but unaware of the device, he set a deadline of midnight. At that point, he'd call Kirk's home number. If there was an answer, and especially if the person on the line seemed calm, sleepy, or unconcerned, he'd have to assume that nothing had yet happened. He'd hang up and assume failure. The plan depended on Kirk coming home tired, annoyed with the non-functioning garage door, annoyed to find something in the way, and thoughtlessly moving it. The same thing might happen in the morning, but the man would have less reason to clear the way then; his car would have been out all night, and he might simply go out the front and drive off. If that was the case, Belonwu would have to decide: leave the device and hope Friday night would be better (worse, of course, from Kirk's perspective), or try to recover it, unfired, during the day. He had to get it back, one way or the other; unlike a bomb, it didn't destroy itself when it was triggered. There'd be lots of evidence and no real chance that Belonwu could see for a second try.

He knew that what he should be hoping was that he'd find the whole thing had worked, that he'd show up behind the house in the dark hours, and the lights he'd noted were on. That would be an indication that Kirk had come in, turned at least the garage lights on, and then set off the device. If the lights were off, well, it could mean that Kirk hadn't been home or that he had been, didn't find the device, and had gone to bed. That he'd get inside safely and not at least turn on the kitchen lights seemed unlikely.

And so he waited and turned the outcomes over and over. Periodically, he'd wince as he got to the part where Kirk was shot and lay dying there on the dusty floor of the garage. The professor was unknown; Belonwu had never seen him, only once heard his voice on the phone. There was no grudge, no animus, nothing but a simple necessity. Kirk had to die so that Belonwu wouldn't be killed by thugs or terrorists or the Nigerian police. His view of Nigeria was out of focus, seen through the cloudy light of western and African journalism. He knew or thought he knew that it was full of people who would kill for wealth or kidnap for it, one being as bad as the other from his standpoint. He believed that people of Nigerian origin who came back to the country from the US were mistrusted, disliked, and targeted, called 'Americanah' and regarded mostly as funding sources. If he got there, he thought, and there was any suggestion that he'd come to find and remove a treasure, he might as well wear a giant 'kick me' sign.

Obviously, his notions of what would happen in Africa were dim, at best. How would he get into the target house? Certainly not through a simple garage door. Some of the family, whoever they were, would be there. Maybe several families lived there. Could he possibly claim to be a repairman, someone come to look at the gas line or the plumbing? Did they have a gas line? Did they have plumbing? What would a man who couldn't speak anything but English say that would get him into a stranger's house, into a specific room, and then be left alone to make holes in the wall? Would the people be Igbo or Hausa, Christian or Muslim? It was insane, completely insane. But here he was, walking now from the cafe to the library, listening to police radio, waiting to see if his plot to murder a stranger had worked or failed. How much more insane could anything else be, by comparison? "*At least,*" he thought, "*if I get to Nigeria, I may be killed, but I probably won't have to kill anyone myself.*" He clinched his jaw in an unconscious technique to regain focus. Tonight was enough. Worry about tonight.

At a quarter after twelve, he drove slowly past the little park behind Kirk's house. To get there, he'd gone by the end of Kirk's street, and there were no police cars or ambulances, no activity at all that could be seen. He drove with his lights on and at a normal pace, slowing without touching the brakes as he reached the park. No one was there, that he could see, and the nearest streetlight was far enough down the block to give the small green space only a kind of dim twilight. In other places, a small darkened playground might be a risky place to be, after midnight. Here, it was just a patch of grass and a few swings; it was supposed to be deserted at night, and in fact, it was.

Belonwu continued on to the end of the block, turned right, and circled back. Before turning down the same street again, he shut off his headlights. When he reached the park, he put the car in neutral and brought it to a stop with the emergency brake. Many years ago, the connection that would have turned the brake lights on had failed, dissolved by road salt. He shut off the engine, turned the dome light off, and got out. A new set of gloves and a new pair of lab booties were already in his pockets, the others and the super glue disposed of in a municipal garbage can. He had his kitchen knife still, and if anyone had searched him, his gear would have seemed fairly suspicious. But he relied on his car and his judicious driving; no police officer had taken a second look.

He went through the park using the darkest side, and moved part way through the gap in the hedge. Through the door wall, the lights in the kitchen lit up the deck and part of the yard. Better still, the garage lights were on, shining through the open back door and its window. Belonwu drew in a breath and walked quickly across the open ground, past a large tree, and up to the back wall, just to the right of the door. There was a faint smell of black powder. He looked in the door.

Fifteen minutes later, he was back in his car. The device sat on the back seat. Automatically, he turned the ignition key, released the parking brake, and let the car slip gradually away, the idling engine turning the transmission slowly in the lowest gear. His hands were tight on the steering wheel, and he swallowed repeatedly, trying to keep from being sick. He felt not at all like a warrior, he was exhausted, and he had an absolutely damning piece of evidence in plain sight in the back of his car.

There was, of course, a plan for what had to happen next. He had to get that thing, heavy with its iron supports and the dead weight of its empty revolvers, out of his possession. And he knew how he planned to do it. Marked on his phone's map application was a spot on a rural road, west of Pinckney, a lonely stretch with no houses, no lights, and woods on both sides. There was a place where he'd decided you could pull over and carry something across the ditch and into the woods and there'd be no reason anyone would ever see it, not until weather and rust had rendered it untraceable. He'd found the road on one of his estate auction expeditions, and it was where he meant to take the device and consign it to the countryside. He let the phone give instructions, and he concentrated on keeping his driving legal and unexceptional.

Because it was late, he reasoned that highways and major streets were safer. If he could just keep the fear and the nausea and the cups of coffee he'd had from disturbing his focus, he should be able to blend in with the traffic on M-23 and then with the smaller volume of people using M-36. Once out there in the backwoods, he shouldn't see anybody at all. (He was, after all, city-raised. Livingston County was backwoods to him.)

Slowly, he regained control of himself. He hadn't considered what a murder scene would look like, hadn't imagined anything of the details, the blood on the device, the blood on the floor, the body half in and half out of the house. The plan had worked, all right, and a large part of Belonwu's consciousness wished emphatically that it hadn't. But it had, and there was just one task more in this first phase of the plan. In the next phase, it was merely his own life he'd be risking, and somehow there was comfort in that.

When the phone told him to, he slowed down and turned south off the two lane highway. This road was barely two lanes wide, unpaved and deserted. A few yards beyond a wavy arrow sign—'winding road ahead'— he stopped. In front and behind, there was nothing but the tan gravel of the road; the woods on either side were pitch black. He shut off the lights and stepped out of the car. As he did, the trees in front of him suddenly started to glow. There was the crunching sound of wheels, and a pair of headlights came over a slight rise, dipped back down, and lit up Belonwu and his car like daylight.

He froze, unable to process what was happening. The lights came on, edging over to get past on the narrow road. He thought for a moment that they'd just go by, but they slowed down and stopped. The pair of lights became a vehicle, a full-sized pickup truck. He just stared. The driver's window came down.

"Having any trouble?"

Belonwu's grip on the door handle tightened. His mind suddenly kick started itself; from somewhere, a reserve of capacity, a jolt of survival instinct allowed him to reply, almost in a normal tone of voice.

"No, thanks. I thought I ... I thought a tire was going down. But they're all okay."

"You sure? I can call somebody for you." The driver was a woman, in her late thirties. White. Of course.

"That's all right. Thanks, though. I have a phone. I think, um, the tires are all right. I must have imagined it."

"Need any directions? There's not a lot out here." The implication seemed clear. There wasn't much out here, and there certainly wasn't much reason for someone like Belonwu, in his faded blue sedan, to be here, either. Not at this hour of the night.

"No, really. I'm fine. Thanks for stopping." He got back into his car, turned the lights on, and drove slowly forward. The truck stayed where it was; Belonwu went over the little rise and around a curve, and he lost sight of its lights. He was as close to outright panic now as he'd been all night.

There are parts of southeastern Michigan where diversity is embraced, where the differences among people are welcomed and cherished as part of the human experience that makes us all one. This was not one of those places. *Oh shit, shit, shit!* he thought. *I'm out here in the woods at ...* He glanced at his phone. *Two-fifteen in the morning, out of my car, and for Christ's sweet sake, I'm black! She just saw a black guy doing something weird! She had a phone! She'll call it in! She has to! There's no way off this road! It just runs down ...* He looked at the phone again. *South! Just south! And then it's miles back east to the highway! What'll I do if they stop me? What'll I say?* The device, silent and damning, still sat on the back seat.

Two things were operating in Belonwu's favor. One thing was that he could drive on autopilot pretty well, even when his mind was fully occupied with other things. He'd had a lot of practice, going back and forth between Ann Arbor and his home in Gardner, letting his reflexes guide the car while his brain turned over some engineering problem or, lately, details of the plan. He managed to keep the car on the road and down at a legal speed as he tried to figure out what the hell to do next.

The other thing was just plain old luck. His analysis of the situation was reasonable, given the conditions of the encounter and the demographics of this part of the state, but very fortunately for him, the woman who'd stopped had a non-traditional view of the world. She was a nurse, headed for a very late shift at a distant urban hospital, a shift in the emergency room. Five nights out of seven, she got up in the small hours, dressed, and headed out from her lakeside house, hers after an unpleasant divorce. At home, her two children and her mother slept on. Of course, she was surprised to see another car on that remote road, even more surprised to see it stopped and the driver standing beside it. That he wasn't a Caucasian, though, didn't make an impression. Her patients were all over the ethnic map, and instead of categorizing them as black, white, Hispanic, and so on, she grouped them into behavioral clusters: cooperative, uncooperative, violent, delusional, intoxicated, conscious, unconscious. Those who weren't a physical threat and were prepared to accept patiently the care she could offer were fine with her. She dealt with straight men, gay men, straight men in women's clothing, straight women with acute alcohol poisoning, skinheads with knife wounds, children with bruises and cigarette burns. For her, humanity fell very neatly into two clumps: the reasonable and the unreasonable. This young fellow standing beside his car had appeared to be reasonable. He'd even said, "Thanks", a word she didn't hear all that often.

It didn't mean she wasn't curious, though. She stepped out of the truck with a flashlight, a big heavy one that she carried with her in the hospital employee parking lot, and shone its beam into the greenery where Belonwu's car had been stopped. Instantly, the light was reflected from a metallic surface. She observed what you can observe on the side of virtually any road, anywhere in the state: a beer can. The mystery was cleared up. That young man had been, probably in more ways than one, getting rid of his beer. She got back into her pickup and went on to work.

Meanwhile Belonwu fled, in a legal and conscientious manner, from an imaginary pursuit. As soon as he could, he turned off his dirt road onto a paved two-lane. It took him through a small town, really just a couple of bars and a tourist trap. Now, after closing time, the lights were off and the parking lots mostly empty. He was so focused on detecting any possible police presence that he missed the irony: it was the coyly-named hamlet of Hell, Michigan.

He turned right the first time an opportunity offered and began to feel better about his chances. Any cop getting a call about suspicious behavior at the place he'd been wouldn't assume that the suspicious person would be going this way, southeast and vaguely in the direction of Dexter. They'd assume (or he desperately hoped they'd assume) a route back east to M-23. It took forever, and the darkness and the sheer rural emptiness of the countryside were fearful, but he made his way, finally, back to the suburban world, getting on I-94 seven miles or so to the west of Ann Arbor.

Now what? He still had to unload the thing. He had to get some sleep. Eating something would be smart, too, although he had no appetite. And daylight was coming on; the device was still sitting back there behind him, uncovered, unexplainable. There was a blanket in the trunk, kept in the car as part of a snow-emergency kit he'd once started to assemble. The first thing to do would be pull off somewhere and cover the thing. With that in mind, he left the freeway at the next exit, executed the Michigan left turn (a mandatory U-turn; you turn right, get over into the left lane, and when traffic permits, you reverse course in order to go the way you really wanted to), and began looking for a business that would be closed and unlikely to have security cameras in place.

Once he had the thing covered, he didn't dare stay put. He went back out onto Jackson Road and kept going east. He had to stop driving somewhere, had to think, had to be out of the way, out of traffic, off the road, before his frayed nerves broke down completely. As he passed a strip mall, a Coney Island turned its lights on, beckoning the early breakfast trade. That would do; he'd never been out on this side of town, and no one would know him. He used first one and then another of the turnaround lanes to circle back and pull in.

He still wasn't hungry, but he had enough sense to eat before he put any more coffee in his system. He ordered a couple of scrambled eggs and some toast and tried to think. Every path he took led to the same constants: he had to get the device out of his car and out of his life as soon as possible, and he had to accomplish that without being seen doing so. There was no chance of that by taking it home to his apartment; the trash bin was right under a security camera, set up to prevent people breaking into cars in the small lot. There was no place in the apartment where his roommate wouldn't see it. The sun was up now, and the thought of going back out into the country was terrifying, day or night. If he didn't blend in, he didn't want to be there.

So that left just one option; he looked at his watch and saw that it was six-forty-five already. In forty minutes, he could be at his parents' house in Gardner. His father left for work at seven-fifteen, and his mother usually went out to a gym a bit after that. If he left now, he might be able to get there during the window when they'd both be away, and he could take the device downstairs. Then, if he took off the stained and punctured covering and dismounted the guns, he could take them away again, concealed in a box or a suitcase or something and carried in the trunk. At least then a simple traffic stop wouldn't unquestionably be a disaster. He'd leave the frame of the device in the basement for a day or so, and he could explain it somehow, if he had to. He could claim it was a project for some class.

He paid his bill and got back on the road, doubling back west once more to get on the highway; he went east on I-94 again, heading toward Detroit and the suburbs. Belonwu was relieved to have a plan, even if it meant relying on his parents' consistency; at least it was a plan, and he let his mind slide gradually away from scheming, just staying alert enough to run with traffic. He drove in a state of trance almost as far as Metro Airport before a billboard with a digital clock reminded him of the time. His brain jumped from time to date and then to the day of the week. "Son of a bitch! It's Friday!"

His stomach cramped up. Friday! His father was a financial drone at a company with government contracts. For reasons Belonwu never understood, Dad worked a five-day week and then a four-day week, nine hours a day, and then had every other Friday off. And this was an off Friday! He remembered his father talking about staying home and doing some painting or some repairs or something, some chore that would keep him there all day! Damn it!

Just as the magnitude of this obstacle hit him, he passed a Wayne County Deputy, sitting on the side of the road with a car pulled over. The flashing lights pushed Belonwu over toward panic again, and almost without knowing he was doing it, he signaled and took the exit that suddenly appeared. He didn't mean to, and he had no idea what he would do now, but he slowed down, and as he came to the end of the off ramp, the traffic light there turned green. He was in the left lane, so he turned left and found himself driving under the freeway. Ahead, a green and white sign said 'I-94 West Ann Arbor Chicago' with a left arrow. He turned left again, merged somehow into the growing stream of traffic, and headed back the way he came.

Belonwu was a student in Ann Arbor with a student's limited concern for traffic and commute times and for alternate routes. When he was calm and rested, he knew enough to avoid certain streets at certain times, but it wasn't a matter of deep concern. He didn't send messages to his council members, complaining about congestion and street closures (he didn't actually know who his council members were). Now that lack of tactical knowledge was about to bite him.

There are two ways, in general, to get into Ann Arbor from I-94, going west. You can go up M-23 to the north for one exit and then go into town on Washtenaw Avenue. Half the people who work in Ann Arbor but live elsewhere will be doing the same thing on a weekday morning. The other way is to stay on the Interstate and get off at State Street; most of the remaining commuters will be joining you on this route. Neither State nor Washtenaw is engineered for the volume of traffic they have to handle; the people trying to get downtown or to the eastern parts of the university pack Washtenaw Avenue. The employees of the huge mall on South State Street and the businesses that surround it, plus another large segment of university people will be there, competing with you for that path. On the north and west sides, there are similar chokepoints. By the time Belonwu had driven back past Ypsilanti, traffic was slowing down. It crawled past Michigan Avenue and came to a complete stop a mile short of M-23.

He was horrified. Even though he had no plan at all, other than a stupid and desperate idea that he'd just go home and leave the device in his car, he still wanted this whole thing to be over. He wanted out. He needed to sleep and think and stop looking over his shoulder. The traffic was just another obstacle thrown in his way, another frustration. His eyes began to tear up.

In fact, at least as far as the police were concerned, he was safer than he'd been in hours. No cop in his right mind would execute a traffic stop out here; if you created more delay, people would just get crazier, and someone would do something really stupid, something like driving down the shoulder or getting out and starting a fist fight. And for sure, nobody was speeding. Nor was there anything to be done about the holdup; there wasn't an accident, no terrorist incident, just simple overflow. The exits here were just not able to handle traffic above a certain volume, especially traffic with semi-trucks mixed in. There was nothing to do but wait it out.

And that was what Belonwu had to do, along with everyone else grinding their teeth and drinking coffee and talking on their phones. Every time the traffic light at the State Street off-ramp turned green, a handful of cars and trucks moved off. Sometimes they didn't move very far, but they moved. And the vehicles behind them moved forward with them until the lights turned red. This movement transferred itself back down the westbound lanes, a few car-lengths at a time, and slowly, slowly the pack moved forward. Belonwu was in the right lane, and after twenty minutes, he realized that his lane was going to become the exit for 23, going north. He didn't care. He wanted to get off this damn highway, and it did seem that the right lane was moving slightly faster than the rest, the people who were holding out for State Street. He took the ramp and gradually merged his way into the painfully slow traffic headed for Washtenaw.

From the center of one cloverleaf to the other, the distance from the I-94 interchange to the Washtenaw exit is two miles; it took Belonwu a solid half an hour to get there, stopping and going all the way. Most of the traffic was pointed north along with him, and there were plenty of people on Washtenaw waiting to join in. The interchange was old, designed in an earlier era; the ramp to get off and go west and the ramp to get on and go north were, briefly, the same piece of pavement, meaning that those two flows had to cross each other. Lots of brake-tapping and nervous glancing-over-the-shoulder went on. It was a great place for minor accidents.

Just as he approached the exit lane, a service van of some kind appeared coming up from the street, anxious to get merged in and up to Plymouth road. An SUV ahead of Belonwu, trying to exit, saw the van, freaked out, and twitched away, bouncing its fender off the side of a semi-trailer that happened to be on its left side, minding its own business. The SUV jerked the wheel back to the right, and the van got a piece of it as it tried to squeak by. Then the van over-corrected and got a piece of the guard rail, too. Belonwu braked hard, and it was greatly to the credit of the car behind him that he wasn't rear-ended. Traffic came to a complete stop.

Belonwu's condition at this point was almost beyond description. The very least of his worries was an increasing need to find a restroom. Beyond that, beyond anything else, was just an all-consuming desire to be done with it all. There's no good purpose to be served describing the interminable process of someone calling the police, waiting for the police to fight their way through the traffic, waiting for the police to determine what had happened and which cars had to be towed (in the event, none of them; they were all drivable), waiting for the police to get the cars and drivers out of the way, and waiting for them to let the innocent cars in the exit lane proceed. Belonwu was catatonic by the time he got to crawl, slowly, down the ramp and go west toward town. Somewhere along the way to his apartment, some of his mental capability returned, and all the arguments against going home with the device came back to him. Ahead, the split of Washtenaw and Stadium Boulevard was coming up, but just in front of it was a traffic light, and off to the left and right, residential neighborhoods. For no particular reason, he moved over into the left lane and with the green arrow turned onto a street called Liverpool. He followed it mindlessly, then turned left again, and noticed for the first time that the sidewalks were lined with city garbage bins, standing in front of suburban-looking homes.

Suddenly and without considering it at all, he pulled over and stopped. On his left was a house, similar to the ones on either side. There were two trash bins in front. He got out, opened his back door, and pulled the blanket off the device. He dragged the clumsy object out of the car and, carrying it in the same way Alan Kirk must have, set it down next to a dark blue bin. With no emotion, no feeling at all, he got back in the car and drove away.

... on the Aegean ...

It was one o'clock, and Charlie Blake was hungry. He was used to eating lunch earlier in the day, but this was when His Honor the Mayor could get free of his busy schedule, and so they were going to have lunch now. The restaurant, quite a distance from Gardner, was a family place, no liquor license, big servings of bland food, oversized sandwiches and burgers. There was no dress code for customers, but there was one for people dining with Mayor Polowski: 'Wear a loose shirt and don't tuck it in. No jacket'. Blake didn't question those instructions, since he knew exactly what they implied. The mayor was being looked at by the FBI, after all, and he wanted this particular conversation to be off the record. Blake trusted Polowski as far as he could throw him, and he was aware that Polowski thought the same way about him.

Blake waited in his car until Skootch and his assistant arrived. As agreed, he'd parked behind the building, where a quick examination of his torso, shirt pulled up and out of the way, went unseen by anyone who shouldn't have seen it. It wasn't all that uncommon an event, anyway, at this particular place. The mayor's assistant, a large guy who was fifty percent of the mayor's security team, said "Okay," and told the mayor, "Clean."

Polowski held out his hand, and Blake shook it. "Good to see you again," he said.

As they walked around to the door, another car drove in.

"There's Achilles," said the mayor. "I asked him to come along."

"Fine," said Blake. "We need him, too."

There was a table in a corner, near the kitchen and its ambient noise. Other tables were farther away than they might have been. It was Polowski's usual table, and the waitress brought his usual iced tea right away, without asking. They ordered, and then the mayor kicked things off.

"So you talked to our pals?"

"Yeah, I did," said Blake.

"And?"

"They bought in. Like we talked about."

"So you and I have a talk, and you're carrying equipment? It's all on the record?"

"Yeah."

"You know how it's gotta go? I mean, you come and bitch about your inspections?"

"I say Prine wants to get paid."

"And I say you're nuts, no he doesn't, he never said nothing like that. He wouldn't do that stuff. You got compliance problems, you gotta fix 'em. That's how we do business here. Play by the rules. Nobody takes payoffs."

"And so, maybe we argue about that a bit, but you keep saying there's no, uh, off the table way of doing it."

"And I sound real convincing. And like you're insulting me." The mayor looked at Achilles Gordon. "Then we bring up the parking thing."

"Right," said Blake. "I say, what about the parking club?"

"The Executive Club," said Gordon.

"Uh huh," said Polowski. "And I say, the what? There's no club. What are you talkin' about?"

"And we argue again, and you call Gordon. And he comes up to your office."

"And he says the same thing. There ain't no club, there ain't no special deals. Maybe I say I'm sorry you got a ticket at City Hall, but the law's the law."

Blake knew the script already. "And then I get mad and I walk out."

"Right. And our friends hear it all."

"Yeah. And then I get my permits."

There was silence around the table. Polowski nodded his head, very, very slightly.

Blake took a deep breath. "There's another thing."

"What?" asked the mayor.

"Well, I got this loan. I owe a guy some money."

"So?"

"He's from up north." Blake said the lender's name. It made no impression, or at least none that showed.

"Never heard of him," said the mayor. "What's your point?"

"Well, the Feds ... our friends, I mean, they think there's a connection. With the city."

"Like I said, I don't know this guy. Gordon, you ever hear of him?"

"No," said Gordon.

"Me either," said the security man.

"Okay, I don't know why they think ... I don't know. But I got a problem with him."

"So?"

"It would help me out if you could ... ah, call him, you know, talk to him. Tell him I'm getting the permits thing fixed. I just need a little more ... a little more time." It was Blake's weakest card, and he knew how pathetic it must have sounded. But he had to try. Just getting his permits kicked loose wasn't going to be enough to fix all his credit issues, not by a long shot.

"I'll think about it. After we have our talk. Jack, you got that name?"

"Yeah, I got it." Security wasn't just muscle in the Polowski administration, it was also a kind of walking mental notebook for the mayor. Things he had to keep track of but didn't want to write down, things like the name of a loan shark, were committed to memory by his assistants.

"Good. Thanks, I'd appreciate it. Are we done, then?" Blake asked.

"Yeah, we're done. Call the office to set up the talk, all official and everything. Goes on my calendar, I take notes like I always do, I send you a follow-up letter. All official."

"Great," said Blake, reaching for the bill. "Let me get this."

"You crazy?" said the mayor. "You tryin' to influence public policy? Jack, put it on the card."

Achilles Gordon drove away from the restaurant with things on his mind. He didn't like this arrangement. He didn't like Blake, either. It wasn't personal; he just objected to stupid people who were in a position to foul up his own set of plans. In Gordon's opinion, Charlie Blake qualified as stupid on at least three counts. *One*, he was trying to screw the City of Gardner while trying simultaneously to do business there. The two were not compatible. A business owner is a partner of the city, not a customer. Everybody Gordon had dealt with in the last twenty years knew that.

Two, Blake was trying to screw a connected guy who'd loaned him some money. Gordon had lied as a matter of course about not knowing the lender, but he did; at least, he knew the name. And he was about ninety percent sure the mayor did, too. Blake had been dumb enough to do business with this guy in the first place, and now he was being dumb enough to think he could stretch out some payments? Just on Polowski's say-so? Did he even think Polowski would make that call? No. Not gonna happen. Not normally, and especially not now, not with trouble on the horizon.

And *three*, for Christ's sake, Blake was trying to screw the FBI! The FB Goddam I. They were gonna set him up with a wire and all, thinking they were gonna get juicy stuff on the mayor, and instead they'd hear a nice sermon! A not guilty plea! Moron. The mayor'd do that talk to the Feds in person if it would do any good. Under oath. If Blake thought he'd get his permits just for doing that ... No, Polowski was setting Blake up to get screwed himself, somehow. Bet on it.

Yup, Blake was trouble, and he was trouble at an especially bad time for Gordon. Achilles was close to kicking off a program of his own, one he'd had in the works for a decade, and he was very protective of it. He'd put a lot of time and effort into it. He lived cheaply, kept his head down, and did what he was told, and the money he got out of it had moved quietly overseas, off to that little Greek town on the coast where Mom lived. It was more money than the mayor knew about and certainly more than the IRS knew about, and in less than thirty days, he'd leave on his usual vacation to the old country. He'd fly into Athens, take a local flight to Araxos, his uncle would meet him, and they'd drive to Kato Achaia. The authorities in that economically devastated country were as open to reason as those of Gardner, and their cooperation had already been secured. Achilles wouldn't be making a return flight.

All of that hinged on this damn investigation dragging on for a while. As long as no one made him turn in his passport for just another month, Gardner and everybody else could kiss his ass. He'd be retired in a place with sunshine and decent food and his loving mother, under the wing of friendly and well-compensated officials, and the United States—well, they'd have a hell of a time catching up with him again. But if somebody like Blake got the Feds excited about a connection with, say, loan sharking, they might just be smart enough to ask questions about who had relatives overseas and things like that. Nope, Blake was trouble. Gordon would have to think about that some more, but he already had an idea or two.

... it brought into his mind ...

Saturday morning, the fifteenth of June. Andy had the day off, and he lay awake in bed, trying to make sense of tangled threads. In theory, he was trying to sort out what possible kinds of connections there could be among Gardner, Charles Blake, Blake's wife, her grandfather, her younger brother, and Alan Kirk. Oh, and the CIA. That was a comforting thought; he knew just enough to worry about what he didn't know. What if he went on with the Gardner assignment as just a corruption story, but somehow it turned out to be a murder, too? And a weird murder, a really strange, going-to-a-lot-of-trouble murder. With the CIA thrown in. There'd be news stories, stuff on the web, bloggers and commenters, conspiracy theorists and loonies coming out of the woodwork. He could screw up his own work and, worse, he might screw up Jenn's.

That was the other thing, the other thread he was fussing with and pulling on. Jenn. He'd enjoyed Thursday night as much as he could remember enjoying anything recently. She liked the same things he liked, the same music, the same wine. She claimed not to be a cook, but there was nothing wrong with her appreciation for food. They hadn't gotten to full-disclosure life stories yet, but he knew she'd been married once; he knew she had a pair of grown daughters. He knew he liked her, as much as he'd liked anyone.

He didn't know if she liked him. It seemed she did. She always accepted an invitation. (Okay, four out of four, so far, but still a hundred percent.) There was a reserve, though, a sense of holding back, even a wariness, perhaps? He admitted to himself that Andy Patel, as of the year 2013, didn't really know a damned thing about women, especially grown women with credentials and careers and one marriage down already. As bosses or suspects, yes, he could deal with them. As friends and partners:

that was another matter. He lay there pondering and, as usual when he tried to think in bed, came to no conclusion.

On the other hand, Jenn was up and dressed and working. She had quite a bit of information on Belonwu Mbanugo , his picture, his addresses in Gardner and Ann Arbor, what he was studying, the labs and workshops available to him—a great deal of data, but nothing except his grandfather's name to hook him to Alan Kirk. It was sufficient, though, to drag MacArthur out of bed and get him to skip his usual Farmer's Market trip in favor of a visit to the young man. Mac, with a lifetime of police machismo behind him, didn't think Belonwu would be dangerous; Jenn, with her own ideas about the kind of person crazy enough to make the device, got a patrol officer to go along. The one who got the task was Jeri Klein, not because of her earlier involvement with the case, but simply because she was on duty and available.

It was just nine o'clock when they knocked on the door of Belonwu's apartment. It was part of a house on Arch Street, east of Packard, and an hour or so before, Emily Weiden's morning run had taken her right by it. Before they approached, Mac had taken a quick look at cars in the street and in the small dirt parking lot behind; they knew what kind of car Belonwu had, but nothing on the scene looked like it.

The man who answered the door was clearly not Belonwu. He was white, slender, with some kind of fashionable haircut; it was in disarray from having been slept on, and he himself wasn't happy about being roused out of bed. Jeri Klein was in uniform, Jenn showed him her badge, and she introduced MacArthur as a 'consultant'.

The young man was Belonwu's roommate, a pre-law student named Kevin, and he wasn't one of those young people who suffer from low self-esteem. His self-esteem was just fine, and you could tell that by his approach to life, his conversational style, and his half-baked and fragmentary knowledge of the law. He demanded everybody's name, he wanted to see a warrant. He asserted that without one, they were trespassing. Jenn explained that all they wanted to do was speak with a particular person; she named Belonwu and showed Kevin a picture. Kevin said there was no one else present, it was his apartment, his name was on the lease, and they could come back when they had proper authority to do so.

Mac had been smiling quietly in the background, saying nothing. Now, he spoke up.

"How old did you say you are?"

"What?" said Kevin. "Me?"

"Yeah. I know how old *they* are," said Mac, glancing at his colleagues. "There isn't anybody else here, right?"

"No. I mean, no, there's nobody else here."

"So how old did you say you were?"

"I'm twenty. You want to see my ID?"

"Oh, no," said Mac, "I'll take your word for it. Whose beers are those?" There were, in fact, three unopened cans of lager standing on the kitchen table.

"Now, I don't really care, one way or the other," Mac said, "I'm not interested. But maybe you could reconsider letting my associate here," ... he nodded at Jenn ... "have a quick look in those bedrooms, just to make sure Mr. Mbanugo isn't here. Then we'll get out of your way. Or maybe this officer here, who does care about that sort of thing, could cite you for being a minor in possession."

"That's not my beer!" Kevin said.

"But this is your apartment, right? Didn't you just say that?" Jeri Klein asked. "Your name's on the lease?"

"And you know," said Jenn, "Now that you mention it, Officer Klein, don't you get just a faint smell of marijuana? Maybe from next door, or it could be ..."

138

"Look, I told you my roommate isn't here. If you want to look, fine," said Kevin who, despite being a prick, was smart enough to know when he was outnumbered.

"I'll wait here," said Mac. "I'll make sure nobody drinks your beers."

The bedrooms were both small, and there was nothing in plain sight (unlike the beers) to incriminate anyone. Jenn thanked the young man for his cooperation, and left him her card.

"When Mr. Mbanugo comes home, please have him call me. He's not in trouble, we just want to talk to him. It's really quite important."

Outside, they paused by Jenn's city car; it was a miscellaneous dark color, not black but dark. Klein's patrol car was parked behind it.

"Sanctimonious little bastard," said MacArthur. "He's going to be a lawyer, too. Did you see his books?"

"He'll have to hike up his pants and turn his ball cap around, but otherwise, he's just about there now," said Klein.

"There wasn't anything about the CIA, though? Or Nigeria?" said Jenn. "There was a lot of engineering and math stuff in Mbanugo's room, but no smoking guns. Or non-smoking guns, either."

Mac shook his head. "But you're getting good at that name. Is that how it goes?"

"I'm not positive. That's how Andy ... that's how I heard it."

Inside the house, Kevin peered out the window at the cops. Three of them, still. One in uniform, one a detective, and the guy ... What did she say he was? A *consulting* detective? Bullshit! He was something creepier than that." *And they're getting in a black unmarked car! This whole thing is bullshit!*" The cops were laughing, and one of them was pointing down the street. Kevin could hardly wait for Belonwu to get back from the store!

Outside, Jeri Klein and Jenn were recalling a burglary a few houses away, the one in which their only witness claimed to have seen a suspicious person running pantless down Arch Street. They split up, Jeri going back on patrol and the detectives deciding to check university libraries. Both of them had been out of college for long enough that they could imagine a student being in a library on a Saturday morning. Neither one was going to drive to Gardner that day, anyway, but if they went and chatted with librarians, they might be able to call it working. And they could find out who ran the Engineering School's labs and workshops and who might know about a student building weird things in his spare time. It was a rare treat, getting to trespass on the turf of the university's security department (a group MacArthur had once characterized as an armed amateur theatrical society.)

Klein drove away, heading east and intending to take Tappan back to Hill. She got as far as the point where Arch turned into Oakland when there was an urgent call from Dispatch: a burglary in progress on Greenwood, literally a block away. She backed the patrol car around into a driveway, turned on the lights, and went south. Greenwood was a one-way street running back toward Packard, lined with student houses and brought down to one lane by parked cars. She braked hard when two people came running out into her way, one from one house, one from another. She jumped out of the car. The radio was going nuts with other units joining in; a Saturday morning burglary was a great opportunity for a little fast driving, a little adrenaline in an otherwise quiet shift.

Mid-morning was not really a typical time for home invasions, here or anywhere else, but a professional will always try to find an unexploited niche. Jimmy Landry was a young but relatively professional thief. He'd been responsible for at least half the quick thefts in this naive and frequently intoxicated neighborhood for the last several months. He was not a student, but he looked like one; he lived in his parents' house in Ypsilanti Township, and he spent most of his time in Ann Arbor, blending in. This morning, he'd parked on a side street several blocks away, put on his backpack, and gone for a walk in the neighborhoods. He came down Greenwood, picked a house with at least three visible doors, and tried the one least exposed to view. It was unlocked, and he entered quickly.

Unfortunately for Jimmy, the reason the door was unlocked was that the resident, a physics student from Cleveland, had just gone across the street to see if his friend was feeling better. You wouldn't really call this neighborhood a community, but occasionally the people who lived in the student areas did know each other, and this particular morning, Jimmy had stumbled into one of those unusual situations.

"Some guy just went into your house!" That was all it took. One person called the police, the other went running out the door to do ... something. Intervene. Take action. Confront the situation. Shout, "Dude! That's my laptop!" And Jimmy, having no experience at all with being caught in the act, also ran out the door, carrying the laptop.

That was what was happening as Klein bolted out of her car. The victim pointed at Jimmy and yelled unhelpful advice. Jeri shouted the necessary warnings and the demands for the perpetrator to stop and get on the ground. Jimmy ran as fast and as hard as he could back in the direction he'd come, back toward Packard Street. He could hear Jeri's boots behind him, and that sound and her repeated commands pushed him to a higher level of determination. He was not as out of shape as most petty criminals, and he was neither exhausted yet nor out of breath. Instead of giving up, he kept running and ducked right at the first opportunity, a driveway leading north between houses. Jeri was catching up, and between panting breaths she kept shouting a series of reports on her portable radio. Although the second patrol car on the scene was already stopped on Greenwood, the third and fourth ones diverted to Arch.

Coming out behind the houses, Jimmy ran on into an odd feature of the apartment neighborhoods, a connected and paved set of back yards. What had once been lawns and gardens was now parking space for a population that was larger and had more cars than the people who built these homes originally. It wasn't pretty, but it precluded fences and made it easier to escape from block to block if you had to. Jimmy was taking advantage of it, planning to get out onto the next street and from there into the next back yard parking lot, which he knew from experience was similar. Then, however, as he sprinted for the opening between two of the buildings on Arch, he saw a police car come to a hard stop across it. Gasping now for air and with his heart pounding, he cut sharply right toward a few remaining trees, thinking he'd be able to dodge around in them and break away again.

Too late. Jeri was two steps behind him now and as he turned, she threw her left arm out so that the bicep was even with the back of his neck, twisted hard to the right, and knocked him down. The effect was as though he'd been simultaneously sacked and hit in the neck with a two-by-four. He went onto the ground, face down, exactly as a suspect was supposed to, but Jeri was unable to control her own fall completely, and she landed beside him rather than on him. She still had her sidearm in her right hand, and it went skittering away across the pavement. She and Jimmy got up almost together.

The adrenaline, the chase, the sacking: all of them had an effect on Jimmy not unlike narcotics. At least it made him irrational to the extent of believing that he could still get out of this situation and away. Neither the sirens of arriving cop cars nor the sight of other officers running in from several other directions registered. All he could see was that the person facing him, the person who'd slammed him to the ground, was—a girl! Confusion turned into a misogynic rage, and he swung at her with his right (he was still futilely clutching the laptop with the other hand.) Jeri stepped in toward the blow, felt it go past her left ear, and rendered him harmless. She did that by thrusting up and outward with both arms, deflecting both of his out and away. The laptop, which he was trying to raise, perhaps as a weapon, went flying. Jeri's right knee came up between his legs and struck him in the crotch; her hands went on past his head, closed on it from behind, and pulled his face forward against her bowed forehead, breaking his nose. Jimmy was done. He fell back to the asphalt and lay there, curled around himself, gibbering with pain. Jeri retrieved her Glock and re-holstered it. Another officer rolled Jimmy over and cuffed him. Breaking and entering, larceny, fleeing and eluding, resisting arrest, and assault on a police officer; it had taken Jimmy less than five minutes to collect an impressive array of felony charges, along with abrasions from hitting the pavement, fractures in the cartilage of his septum, and a pair of sore bollocks. He'd also managed to fill the Arch Street neighborhood with a large, noisy, and visible police presence, and that had consequences he couldn't have imagined.

Belonwu had actually been shopping, and he came home down Arch Street as Jenn and Mac and Jeri Klein had gone off in the opposite direction. Seeing open spots in front of the house, he parked there and went inside, just as Jeri was jumping out of her car a block away. His roommate (who had now hidden the beers) began to tell him a self-centered and somewhat incoherent account of the interaction with the cops, just as sirens outside began to get louder and closer. Belonwu went to the window, pulled the rolling shade down, and looked around its edge. For a few seconds, the street was empty. Then all hell broke loose, at least in his perception of it. Patrol cars came down Arch from both directions, and cops leapt out, drawing their weapons and yelling at their radios. Kevin the roommate was still talking, very excited now, and Belonwu's sense of panic was back at the levels it had been, driving around in Livingston County in the dark. He bolted into his bedroom and began grabbing things at random, stuffing them into a backpack. If he'd been the cool agent of adventure he wanted to be, he'd have had an escape kit ready, a scram bag or an AWOL outfit. As it was, he was improvising wildly and trying to remember where in relation to the sides of the house the fire escape ladder would set you down.

He spent no more than sixty seconds on this frantic phase. Nobody was hammering on the door, there were no loudspeakers telling him to come out with his hands up. He went back to the window and noted that the cop cars were still there, but the cops were nowhere to be seen. He took a deep breath and regained some measure of control. Two rational trains of thought emerged. The first was that if these cops were after *him*, they'd gotten the address wrong. Nobody was kicking down the apartment door. The other thought was in the form of a question: *Where are you going to go?*

Over the remaining time it took the police to corral Jimmy Landry, get back in their cars, and drive away, Belonwu absorbed the story of the detectives' visit from Kevin, colored by Kevin's memory of it and by Kevin's substantial ego. He took careful note of the names and ranks, and he took Jenn's business card. He thanked Kevin for the help and told him it was no big deal; a guy he'd gone to high school with was in trouble, and the authorities were probably looking for him. Probably somebody had said, "He might be crashing with Belonwu." No big deal.

And then, because he'd thought of an answer to the question in that second train of thought, he told Kevin that he had to be away for a few nights, house sitting for a friend. He went back into his bedroom and finished packing a few more items of clothing. He asked Kevin to call him on his cell if the cops came back, and then he went carefully out the door, down the stairs, and away on foot.

Kevin didn't know Belonwu very well. They were luck-of-the-draw roommates, not friends, and they lived together only for economic reasons; they split the rent and the utilities and from time to time shared a pizza. Now he considered his roommate's story, his reactions to the cop visit and the cops outside, his sudden departure. Kevin came to a quick conclusion: "Bullshit!"

As soon as Belonwu got out of sight of the house, he switched directions. He didn't want anyone, the police, Kevin, or anyone else, even to know which way he'd gone let alone where he was going. He put his ear buds in and started the radio scanner application on his phone. There was still chatter, but listening in on the wrap up of an event didn't provide much hard data. It was like listening to the last act of a play, blindfolded, and trying to intuit the plot. He heard nothing about murder, nothing about Alan Kirk; there was talk about a subject, and that subject was in custody. He wondered if perhaps it hadn't been about him. Somehow, some plain clothes officers had shown up asking about him, and then somehow something else had taken place. He wanted to believe it, but right in the neighborhood? With cops parking in front of his house? Could they possibly have arrested somebody else by mistake, someone who looked like him? He doubted it, but still, no one was pursuing him. No patrol cars were cruising the streets as he walked along, his cap stuffed in his backpack and the hood of his sweatshirt up.

What he'd told Kevin was an exaggeration but not quite a pure lie. He'd been given a key to a friend's apartment and asked, not to house sit, but just to drop in and water the plants. The friend was going away for several weeks, and Belonwu decided to use the place for a few days, being very tidy, sleeping on the couch, leaving as little trace of himself as he could. Now that the authorities had his name, he couldn't go back to Arch Street or home to Gardner. He'd have to disappear, 'go covert', as he thought of it. It wouldn't be long, just a few days. Just long enough to find out as much as he could about this detective—he looked quickly at Jenn's card—this Jennifer Langton of the Ann Arbor Police Department, and the mysterious other person who acted like a policeman but who didn't leave a card. MacArthur. Yes, he'd have to find out who MacArthur was and who he was working for. They'd found Belonwu too quickly; there had to be someone else besides just the Ann Arbor Police in the mix. Another agency. Belonwu had a sudden thought, a flash of insight about what that agency might be.

... sweet is the night-air ...

For most of the time they'd been married, Mac and Colleen had had some kind of regular dining-out ritual. For a while, they'd been habitués of a particular downtown bar, the one where they'd more or less met. There'd been a Mediterranean place for a while, with a quirky menu of Italian food. This basement bistro was run by a Greek, one of Ann Arbor's serial restaurant-openers. It closed as his places seemed to do on a three-year schedule, and the MacArthurs had to find a new default spot. While it lasted, they'd been fond of an exposed-brick, country French restaurant in the Kerrytown buildings, but it vanished in a rent-hike dispute with the landlord.

By the beginning of the twenty-first century, they'd settled in as weekend regulars at a comforting, quiet Japanese establishment, a place with an *izakaya* feeling, but a menu of greater ambition. Although the *nigiri* and *sashimi* selections didn't vary with any frequency (they were dictated by the fish you can get flown into the Midwest), the quality was far beyond the pale local competition, and Mac was damned if was going to drive clear down to Flat Rock for a little raw fish. Instead, at least once a week, they drove east, going outside the city walls (that is, under one of the freeways that ring the town like Vauban-style fortifications) using the *Porte d'Ypsilanti* (the underpass that takes Washtenaw Avenue below M-23), and then just half a block north, past the Sheriff's Department.

On this particular Sunday, they arrived in Colleen's car, parked it so as to get back out onto Hogback Road without having to back and fill in the small lot, and walked in for their seven-thirty reservation. They were greeted with the usual smiles and familiarity, and they were seated at their usual spot, one of two or three booths in a quieter part of the dining room. It had taken a long time to settle on a standard drink with their meals; they'd worked through the small wine list and then gone through a period of drinking Kirin lager, but they'd finally identified one of Ozeki's imported sakes as a favorite and a good match for the dishes they usually ate. The staff now routinely brought the small bottle and a pair of glasses with only a nod from Mac.

Ordering was similarly easy; they asked for a few pieces of individual *nigiri* sushi, a special roll, some *agedashi* tofu and a favorite of Mac's, grilled yellowtail jaw meat. With that out of the way, they began to brief each other on current events, Colleen talking about what she was doing to thwart a competitor's assault on one of her larger clients, Mac talking about the Kirk case, spiced with the hints that were recently observable concerning Jenn and Andy.

"She doesn't talk about him in detail, but she keeps saying *Andy said this*, and *Andy mentioned that*."

"But you said there's a hook between his case and hers, right?" said Colleen. "They have reason to be talking, don't they?"

"Sure. No doubt. But it's as though she's catching herself. She'll start to say *Andy said* ... and then she'll change it to *I was told* ... or something."

"It'd be interesting to hear him on the subject of her. Is the FBI allowed to go on dates?"

"I think so, but only in compliance with generally accepted accounting principles."

"All bags are subject to search."

"That's the TSA."

Mac paused to pull another bite off the yellowtail. Colleen refilled his sake glass. "So you didn't get to talk to the student? The one you and Jenn went looking for?"

"No," said Mac, "He wasn't there. So we went off to see if people on campus knew anything about him. We kind of secretly hoped we'd just run into him, crossing the Diag."

"No luck, though?"

"Nah. But Jeri Klein got lucky. Did you meet her? Black woman, tall. She's a uniform."

"I think so. I think you introduced me."

"She was the backup we took with us to Mbanugo's apartment. Literally seconds ... like, ten seconds ... after we get done with that, there's a burglary call from the next street over. She gets there first, runs the guy down. He tries to fight, and she kicks him in the groin and breaks his nose. Turns out, he's probably been stealing stuff in studentville for months."

"Wow."

"They're charging him with about forty-six different things. Jenn and half the other detectives get to clear cases. It was great."

"Will he file a complaint about her using force on him?"

"It's not exactly filing a complaint, but it's something like that. Yeah, his defense probably will try it out, but it won't fly. Two other officers and a witness saw him take a swing at her first. He's screwed."

If Belonwu could have heard this conversation, he'd have been relieved. He'd have known that the brouhaha on Arch Street was not related to him, and even Mac's summary of the fruitless day spent seeking him had a casual note. Yes, they wanted him, but so far the intensity of their desire didn't amount to an around-the-clock manhunt.

He couldn't hear it, even though he was nearby, since his expertise didn't extend to electronic surveillance. Instead, he was in the parking lot, sitting in his friend's car, waiting to see what MacArthur was doing and who he might be meeting. As far as he could tell, the answer was uninteresting; Mac seemed to be dining with his wife or at least the woman who lived at his house. Belonwu had casually walked by the windows, just another person going to or from his car, and he'd confirmed that the two were seated by themselves. Since he knew Mac had a picture of him, he didn't dare go inside. Instead, he'd stay out here, hoping no one noticed a man sitting alone in a car, and he'd wait to see where MacArthur went next.

Belonwu was aware of his vulnerabilities. His own car was still parked on Arch Street, and it would have to stay there now. If the people hunting for him were any good at all, they'd have someone watching it, certainly someone watching the apartment. But for one or two specific, local tasks, things that wouldn't run up many miles on the odometer, he allowed himself to borrow the car of his absent friend. That person had obligingly left the keys, although without an overt invitation to use it. It was in good shape, better than his own car, and so if he drove carefully, he wouldn't be likely to make accidental contact with the police. Of course, if a real accident happened, he'd be in instant trouble. The only license he had to offer was one with his real name on it. The notion of driving carefully took on even greater meaning.

The risk, though, had to be accepted. He'd spent most of yesterday digging into the Internet, trying to gather intelligence on the enemy. He'd proven to his own satisfaction that Langton was what her business card said she was: an AAPD detective. Her name was on the department's website. MacArthur, though, was a different animal. There were news stories from several years ago, quoting a Detective MacArthur of the Ann Arbor Police Department on some minor crime topic. But those references weren't any more recent than 2009, and since then, he had not appeared. His name wasn't on the Ann Arbor website at all.

The FBI's web presence was no real help. There was nothing to be found about MacArthur there, and there was less than nothing at the CIA. As far as the publically-available data that was online, Mac did not exist. None of that, unfortunately, did anything to lesson Belonwu's certainty that Mac was a Fed. *Of course*, the name of someone acting covertly wouldn't be on a list of employees. It wouldn't show up in the local press when they covered a professor's murder or when the man was named 'Secret Agent of the Month'. There wouldn't be pictures of him shaking hands with the President of Nigeria or addressing a Young Republicans meeting in Kabul. Belonwu was familiar with the principle that absence of evidence is not evidence of absence, but he missed the corollary: absence of evidence of spookiness is not evidence of being a spook. He didn't accept that MacArthur could be just an old, retired detective with a coincidental interest in Dr. Kirk. That would be absurd. Belonwu's dying grandfather was connected to the CIA; that connection had brought about Kirk's death; therefore, the CIA had someone looking into it. To this suffering, guilt-stricken young man, that theory made sense, and nothing else did.

Inside, Mac and Colleen finished their meals and their bottle. He'd been on his feet for a good part of the day, more than usual, and he was stiff in most of the joints from his hips on down. That, combined with the sake, left him a bit unsteady, and as they came out of the restaurant, he stumbled slightly, catching the toe of his shoe on the edge of a paving block. Colleen had her arm locked through his, and she steadied him. They paused, then went on to the car, Mac limping as he always did but more noticeably now. He got into the passenger's side, boosting his right leg in with his hand. Colleen shut the door for him. None of this was unusual, and it lasted only a few seconds, but Belonwu saw it and took note.

At home, they greeted the dogs and gave them a final evening's opportunity to go outside. They cleared up in the kitchen, put things away, and waited for the dogs to come back in. Mac went upstairs for his last pills of the day, and Colleen shut down lights on the first floor. In an hour, all four of the MacArthur pack were asleep, two humans in the bed, two dogs arranged around the bedroom floor.

Outside, a car idled slowly by, lights off. Belonwu appreciated the darkness and the trees; they gave a sense of concealment, and helped him accept the risk of running blacked out. It was highly suspicious behavior, but back here in Mac's neighborhood there was almost no one to notice. He stared hard at the house as he went by, committing it to memory, as much of it as he could see. Once around the corner, he turned the headlights back on and drove slowly back to the friend's house. He was thinking hard all the way.

Upstairs, MacArthur was asleep and well into a dream. He was in an old city, with cobblestones under foot. It was dark, and gas lights were burning, giving tremendous atmosphere but not a great deal of illumination. He was going somewhere, walking, and he had a cane in his right hand. It rattled on the pavement with each step. In reality, he'd have been staggering, tripping on the uneven stones. But in the dream, he glided along, and his feet seemed to conform to the surface, as though his boots were soled with some thick flexible material. The storefronts advertised strange products and services, things that made no real sense but still managed to fit with the theme. He wasn't lost, he knew which turns to take and even how far he had to go, but *where* he was going, he couldn't have said.

As he walked, he heard hoof beats on the stones behind him: a shod horse, pulling something, a vehicle with iron-bound wheels. It came up slowly, then suddenly the horse was whipped into a gallop, and it dashed by him, it was a carriage, driven by a bearded man in a top hat. It went ahead by just a building or two and then someone inside threw an object off to the right, off toward the opposite side of the street. The cab rushed on, the window of a shop shattered, and a slow, muted explosion occurred. Policemen with mustaches and peaked helmets ran up, blowing whistles. A horse drawn fire brigade arrived. Suddenly, Mac knew where he had to go. He touched a policeman's arm.

"Excuse me. Which way to the colonial office?"

The policeman looked at him, and he seemed to be weeping. "I'm sorry, sir," he said. "It's on fire."

Mac woke up, aware that his leg had cramped up. He swore quietly and swung out of bed. Standing up and stretching was the quickest way to get the cramp to go away. He limped into the bathroom (narrowly avoiding a sleeping dog) and stood with his hands braced against the counter, the right leg back. He slowly stretched the calf muscle. The dream was already almost forgotten, and all he could reconstruct was a sense that it had been weird. Really only half awake, he was prone to free association, and the thought of weirdness and being in a weird city made him think of the bumper stickers that said 'Keep Austin Weird'. That brought him on to other versions of the same thing, variations he'd thought of: 'Keep Albuquerque Quirky' or even 'Keep Standish Outlandish'. And then he thought, very vividly, of the device with its wrought iron legs and black powder revolvers. Weird, sure enough.

"The brain is a strange thing," he thought. *"And speaking of weird cities, I wonder if Ann Arbor is getting weird again."* It used to be. He realized that he missed it.

... the waves draw back ...

Morning, Monday, June seventeenth. Mac got dressed and prepared to head out for coffee and a stop at a pharmacy. He went out into the backyard and said good morning to the dogs who had had their excitement already, running a squirrel off the property. Mac's appearance on the deck wound them up slightly; most mornings, he was prepared to throw a ball or a stick or take part in a bit of tug. This morning though, he had *snacks*, inch-wide pieces of cold steak, cut from Saturday's leftovers. For steak bits, Snacker and Goose were quite willing to come inside after a bite and a pat on the head. Colleen of course was out of the house already, off to work. He shut and latched the back door, and told the dogs to watch the house. "I'll be back," he told them.

Both of the Shepherds made strong eye contact when Mac was talking, and while they may not have understood what he was saying in the human sense of that term, the repetition in both the words and the tone of voice conveyed useful information. They understood he was going out for a while and they weren't. They knew he'd return and perform his next truly important function of the day, giving them their dinner. But until one or the other of the humans did come back, the house was theirs, in terms both of possession and responsibility.

It's difficult for humans to talk about non-human mental processes. (It's difficult enough to create exposition in a work of adult fiction, when the character is a dog.) What very, very little we know about the mentalities and psychologies of other species suggests that some of the things our own minds do may have parallels in those of certain animals. Whether those parallels really are rare—whether, for example, dogs think the way we do in just a small number of ways—or whether those are simply the ones we've managed to detect so far is probably something that will always be in doubt, right up to the point where community colleges are able to provide night courses in speaking Schnauzer. Until then, when we look a dog in the eye, we'll have to rely on our own experience with the

151

specific dog and on our own stock of anecdotal evidence as we ask ourselves the question (perhaps after the dog has destroyed a supposedly chew-proof cushion or chased the newspaper boy up a tree), "What was he thinking?"

That dogs *don't* think, that everything they do is the product of some mystical construct called 'instinct', is a view still held by some people, but the evidence against it is piling up. Few owners believe it, at least not those who own working breed dogs. We know that dogs certainly seem to have a concept of self, a knowledge of right and wrong, a grasp of fair play and equity, and perhaps even the notion of other entities' points of view. In the last ten years, all of that has been demonstrated experimentally; hell, for publicity purposes, dogs have even been taught to drive a car (admittedly, only with an automatic transmission). But we don't know whether they have a philosophy. It does seem clear, though, that certain dogs have an idea of their place in the universe or, to narrow it down a bit, their reason for existing. In the case of the dogs bred for herding, had there been a canine Jean Paul Sartre, his or her seminal work would not have been *Les chemins de la liberté* but a more direct *Sentiers à la sécurité:* Trails to Security. Herding dogs, when they have nothing to herd, guard. It also seems true enough that with these dogs, existence precedes essence. As the dog grows older, a kind of maturation appears to take place. A Shepherd, for example, that in puppyhood loved and welcomed everybody, dog or human, grows up to behavior patterns that look to a human observer like a mature adjustment to a career and a self: if there had been a Shepherd Descartes, he would have said 'I guard, therefore I am'.

Mac went out via the garage, backing the truck out and using a remote to close the garage door. Snacker padded slowly up the stairs to the second floor and took up a position where she could lie down comfortably. From that point, she could still keep an eye on the front yard and one or two houses' worth of the street. Goose clambered up onto a big upholstered chair in the front room. He curled himself around so his chin sat on one of the armrests; from this position, he could see out the large front windows, and both the front door and the garage entry door were in sight. The only other vulnerability was the backyard door wall, and any approach there would announce itself by sound instantly. He had very good ears. Positioned tactically, both dogs settled down and shortly went to sleep.

Belonwu parked the car on a cross street where he could see both the possible exits from Mac's neighborhood. He was nervous, breathing hard. Things had gotten desperately out of hand, and he could no longer see a clear-cut resolution to anything. His original plan, the starting point, was already receding in his imagination. Having silenced the professor and made sure that no one else knew about the diamonds now seemed unimportant. What mattered most at this point was stopping or thwarting or slowing down the work of the police, the police and whoever this unusual man was, this man who was some kind of official, for sure. An enemy.

He waited, trying to stay calm, and was rewarded with the sight of MacArthur's truck turning out of the nearer of the residential streets. It turned away from him and headed toward Packard. He watched it until it was out of sight, then started the car and turned into the neighborhood. He drove past MacArthur's house and stopped two doors down near the end of the very short block.

Sitting in a parked car on a major street is one thing, but on a tiny street like this, it wouldn't do. This was a very isolated neighborhood, and there would be no reason for a stranger to be sitting here, to be here at all, unless he had some business. There was no time to hesitate; he would have just as much time as it took to walk up to MacArthur's front door to make up his mind.

Another violent death would be extremely undesirable. Anything he did that drew further attention would bring greater focus, more resources, a much greater police effort to find Belonwu himself. As he left the car, he had no weapon, no explosives, no elaborate booby trap. Instead, he had what he hoped was a biological solution. The night before, he'd walked quietly around the study carrels in the graduate library, watching and listening for students who exhibited the most egregious symptoms of influenza. He picked two whose coughing and sneezing made them seem near death. When they left, he used tissue paper to wipe down the desk surfaces they'd just vacated. Later, he soaked that tissue paper in the small bottle of water he was carrying. This MacArthur person, probably some kind of agent, certainly someone who was a threat to Belonwu, was also an older man. He moved slowly and with a limp, and Belonwu had seen his wife keep him from falling, outside the restaurant. To Belonwu, MacArthur looked and acted fragile. A bad case of flu might not kill him, but it could slow him down. It could buy time during which Belonwu could get out of Ann Arbor, away from a place where every cop had his picture and his name. As for administering the virus, there would be something in the refrigerator into which he could pour a bit of the water. He'd pick something generic, milk perhaps, something that both the man and his wife would drink or eat. It wasn't much of a plan, but at this point it was all he had.

He walked up to the door; it was set back slightly, under a small square roof. There was a deadbolt separate from the doorknob, and the only other thing Belonwu was carrying besides the hypothetical virus water was a set of lock picks. As he started to take them out of his pocket, a movement to his right caused him to spin and freeze. Most of the front wall to the right of the door was taken up with a large array of windows. They came down to within a couple of feet of the floor, and on the other side of the windows, staring at him with a deep intensity, were four bright, alert brown eyes. Dark, lengthy muzzles. Upright, pointed ears.

Belonwu had not grown up with pets in the home. In his high school years, the neighbors had owned unfriendly, unruly dogs, dogs prone to barking and lunging against the fence. He was not actually afraid of dogs in general, but they made him uncomfortable. And a pair of large, silent, intelligent dogs, encountered unexpectedly like this, was the last straw. He managed not to drop his burglar tools, turned, and walked back down the steps. Even in Sax Rohmer, one of the genius Doctor's more evil schemes had been thwarted by a simple pack of guard dogs. Now, Belonwu's courage was used up; he was defeated. If the dogs had barked or scratched at the door or showed excitement, it might've been different. But that simple threatening stare was completely unnerving.

Not long after, Mac came home, carrying a caffè latte from the drive-through at Washtenaw and Stadium and a prescription refill. He stumped up the garage steps and unlocked the door, greeted immediately by a pair of noses. "Hi guys," he said, "I'm back." The dogs were in their usual welcome-home state of wag, and Mac produced the requisite pair of small biscuits. "What good dogs," he said. It was a common phrase, just like 'I'll be back' or 'hold the fort', something he and Colleen had gotten into the habit of saying. What the dogs actually thought, expressed in language, was unknowable, on the far side of the chasm of species. But their attitude on this particular morning certainly looked like self-satisfaction. Snacker's reaction in particular might've been translated as, "Good dogs? Yeah, we are, aren't we?"

... neither joy, nor love, nor light ...

Tuesday, June eighteenth. It was the end of the day, but Emily Weiden wasn't finished with the work she'd set for herself as the day's quota. With or without a major professor, she was moving ahead on an outline of the research she intended to do: a clear and fact-based definition of 'right-wing', so that there'd be no quibbling about what it meant; a data structure to collect right-wing groups and movements, along with locations, membership, dates, effect they'd had; and of course, a long, long literature search and bibliography. It was a mountain of work, and at the end it would either support or deny her hypothesis. Emily believed that the number of ultra-conservative groups had grown since the end of the Second World War, but their membership had declined in relationship to the populations from which members might have been drawn. And more than that, she hoped to show that there were patterns and shifts over time, measured as a distance from the war, patterns that would suggest declining effect and withering influence. An acquaintance had suggested a dissertation title: "Are you being a fascist more now but enjoying it less?" Having never seen the Camels ad in question, Emily didn't get the reference.

Regardless, she was tired, and her eyes were sore, and she needed to get outside for half an hour. She changed into the running shoes that she carried back and forth, locked her laptop and purse into her desk, and walked out of the building. She went out a door on the east side and crossed the University Diag, a manicured green space that was roughly if not precisely central to the school's old, original campus. The University of Michigan is one of the state's two huge schools, and unlike its colleague fifty miles northwest, its campuses weren't contiguous. UM property was gathered in two large areas, the Central Campus, here on the east side of downtown, and North Campus, well out of the downtown area in a wedge between Plymouth and Fuller roads. There was a large athletic complex to the south, and other small holdings were scattered around, sometimes quite far away. For Emily, though, Central Campus was the important part. She lived close by, and the Department, the libraries, and a few key administrative locations were all within walking distance.

She could have gone home for dinner and come back, but she preferred home to be *home*, a place she went when the day's work was done. For a break, she liked to cross the Diag, taking (of course) a diagonal route toward North University, then back past Hill Auditorium to State Street. There was always something going on at State, at least in reasonable weather: Christian fundamentalists preaching to the passerby, libertarians urging people to vote against something or other, a descendent of W. H. Auden selling used paperbacks and historically interesting postcards from a sidewalk stand. Tonight, Emily had intended nothing more than to walk this accustomed path.

On this Tuesday evening, there was an obvious set up process underway. All along State and East U people were putting up booths; the roads were closed to cars. Electric cables were being strung out to the sidewalks, and the banners she'd been ignoring for the last few days now made sense: this was the preparation for something the people here called "Art Fair."

The center of the Diag itself was almost empty. The throngs that moved back and forth between class times were gone. Emily had unconsciously adopted a local habit, one that existed because the Diag was such a crossroads. You looked quickly at the people as they passed, checking to see if they were someone you knew, someone you'd want to speak to (or avoid). The big-city practice of refusing eye contact slipped away here. And so when a person came across Emily's path from the left, taking the northwest-to-southeast diagonal walkway, Emily glanced at him.

She almost nodded, since his face was familiar. She'd seen him before in the tiny park on Packard, apparently resting from a run. That had been— oh, Lord!—the day after they found Dr. Kirk. Her stomach knotted up with the thought, and with that thought there was something else. The photo the detectives had showed her! This was him! This was the man they wanted to talk to! Nobody had said 'suspect', but still, this was someone the police wanted to talk to!

She stopped. Nothing in her experience told her what to do. She had her phone; she could call someone. But if she did call, by the time someone got here, he'd be out of sight. Emily was nothing if not decisive; right-wing movements could wait. She would follow this person, find out where he was going, and *then* call the authorities.

Belonwu wasn't watching for young graduate students, he was watching carefully for cops. He assumed that if he stayed away from the Arch Street neighborhood and spent most of his time on campus, a random sighting was unlikely. Obviously, he wasn't attending classes; if the people looking for him had his name, they certainly knew other things, things like his academic major, his class schedule, his professors. So he avoided the Engineering Department and its various buildings, and he even considered that being this close on the Diag was a risk. After all, the southeast exit was through the Engineering Arch, a passage right through the first floor of the Marine Lab. But it was a direct route from places he went to for a few simple supplies, and it was mostly on UM property. The Art Fair set up and the street closures just made it better.

He turned off the diagonal sidewalk and strolled east between Natural Resources and the end of another Engineering building (flipping up his hood, even in the pleasant weather), then on by Pharmacy and Astronomy, and out onto Church Street. He went along beside a parking ramp, past some houses, and onto Washtenaw Avenue.

Emily followed carefully. She had no training in surveillance, and all she knew was that she mustn't lose sight of her target. He didn't seem to be looking back over his shoulder, just ahead. The idea that someone would be following him on foot hadn't occurred to Belonwu. He was focused on auto traffic or people he met who might seem to be interested. Adults. People in uniforms or suits. If he'd turned around and spotted Emily, she wouldn't have fit any of his threat patterns. Emily was just slightly plain, with cheeks that made a pair of lines on either side of her nose. The features of her face were compressed vertically from her eyebrows to her chin, making it seem small in comparison to the size of her head. Her hair was long and deep brown, very straight and pulled back behind her ears.

She wasn't in any sense unattractive, but if you walked into a room, she wouldn't be the first person you'd notice. She might have considered that a drawback, if she'd ever thought about it; today, it was an asset. Nothing about her suggested the word 'nemesis'.

The house where Belonwu was staying was another subdivided residence, this one with only three apartments. It was on one of a pair of traffic-engineering oddities, one-block-long dead end streets, closed off on the north by the city's desire to make a faster and safer street out of Observatory. It made a quarter-circle from Washtenaw (where Belonwu was standing, waiting to cross), and then carried on straight north along a row of dormitories and into the heart of the University Hospital complex. Having multiple residential streets turning right and left onto this sweeping turn was considered a bad idea, and so one end of a street called Wilmot and all of a street called Mack were shut off from Observatory, having their access on Elm. The house of Belonwu's friend was on Mack, and he got there quickly, crossing five lanes with the 'Walk' light, going less than a block farther, stepping off the sidewalk into a parking lot, and then walking another fifty feet to his door.

Emily dogged him, staying as far back as she dared, loitering when he stopped for the traffic light, catching up at a faster pace. When he turned off Observatory, she was momentarily stumped, worried that he'd notice her following that closely. But she had to see where he went, and so she carried on. She watched him go up on the porch of the first house on the left, and when she was sure he had a key out and was using it, she looked away and walked across a grassy area that seemed more or less public, out into another parking lot and back to Washtenaw. In five minutes she was out of sight and using her phone.

... ignorant armies clash by night ...

Belonwu's luggage was as packed as it was going to be. He'd checked repeatedly to be sure he had his passport and a reasonable amount of money. His phone would be useless abroad, but he discovered that phones could be had on the streets, where he was going. Grandfather had given him money, as he'd said he would. Belonwu waited until the last minute to buy his tickets, and he paid for them with an online payment service, not a credit card. It would still be traceable, but he hoped it would take longer. He'd tried again and again to put himself in the place of the people hunting him; would they be expecting him to leave the country? Because of the murder or because of something else? And Nigeria? Would they assume he'd be going there? How much of the story had his grandfather told Kirk? And if Kirk was more than just a professor, how much history had gotten back up the chain? What chain?

The visa was another issue. He'd applied for it as early as he could, well before leaving the device in Kirk's garage. Would that make it harder or easier for the Feds or cops or whoever it was? Would they look for new applications, or would they go back and look at older ones? He had it, anyway, stamped on his otherwise empty passport. If he actually managed to land in Lagos, he should be able to get into the country—if they weren't waiting for him. He'd pondered the choice of outbound airports (Detroit vs. Chicago), and decided on Chicago. It was inconvenient, but it offered another level of indirection. And he could get to Chicago without flying. In addition to his airline arrangements, he had a ticket on an intercity bus from Ann Arbor to O'Hare. A journey of a thousand miles starts with a single step, though, and he hadn't quite worked out the first step.

His bus would leave from Ann Arbor, but when he got around to looking at a map, he realized that it didn't leave from either the local bus stop, downtown on Fourth Street, or the old bus station on Huron. It was a new company whose passengers valued parking as much as schedules, and it had a deal for a place on the south edge of town, two miles from the house on Mack Street. Two miles wasn't all that far, perhaps, but it was more than Belonwu was prepared to walk, carrying luggage, and starting out in the morning.

Annoyed, he called a taxi company; they were booked. He called another, and they explained to him about Art Fair traffic and how they couldn't guarantee anything in terms of pickup time until Saturday evening. They said his best bet would be to walk through the Fair early on, down to Fourth Street, and catch a city bus out to the lot on south State. And so that was his plan for Wednesday, June nineteenth.

Wednesday morning was bright and warm, with the promise of Art Fair weather (either extreme heat and humidity or violent rainstorms, sometimes on the same day.) The night before, Jenn had gotten the call from Emily: Belonwu Mbanugo was living at an address on Mack Street. Jenn had asked the reasonable questions: how did Emily know? She saw him unlock a door at that house, but was she sure he was *living* there? Was she sure it was him?

Emily was very earnest and very correct; she was a little piqued that Jenn was taking time to question her rather than ordering an immediate descent on the house. Jenn explained that Belonwu wasn't even officially a suspect yet, just someone who might have information. But she said she'd go and see about it the next day. Emily heard that as a promise and privately made plans of her own.

On Wednesday, there were other things on Jenn's plate, and it was nearing ten o'clock when she got within a few blocks of Belonwu's temporary house. The problem was that Art Fair was opening, and the nearby neighborhoods were parked up already. She found a place on Wilmot, and she walked around the block to Mack, using her phone to see if there was any kind of backup available. The dispatcher was a friend of Jenn's, and she managed not to laugh. It was Art Fair; nobody was free at the moment. Jenn had considered calling MacArthur, but decided not to. If she found out anything useful, she could brief him later without getting him out in the traffic. And she wasn't sure that he qualified as 'backup', anyway. He moved pretty slowly these days.

She turned the corner onto Mack and walked along it as it bent north toward its dead end. She came around the next-to-last house and stopped abruptly. A young black man with close-cut hair was just walking away toward Observatory, wearing a backpack and carrying a duffle bag. She couldn't see his face, but everything she could see fit Belonwu's description. *Damn it*, she thought, *the grad student spooked him!*

In fact, it was Belonwu, and he wasn't any more spooked than he had been for the last two weeks. He hadn't seen Emily, and he didn't see Jenn now. It was just time to go catch his bus. The day was already too hot for a hoodie or even a hat, and his only concession to disguise was a pair of sunglasses. Everything he had was in the pack or the bag or in pockets of his trousers. He was travelling light on the next step of the great adventure. He turned on Observatory and headed for campus, the most direct way by foot.

Jenn was caught off guard. She had no backup coming, and her car was a block and a half away, parked in a street that was cut off from the one her suspect (she was thinking of him as a suspect, now) was taking. Even if she'd been in her car at that moment, he was heading into the heart of Art Fair, on this day, the most vehicle-unfriendly spot in the state. This was going to be a foot event. She set off after him.

Meanwhile, another person was also watching. She'd been there, sitting in her own car, since six AM. Emily had gotten up early, dressed and eaten, and armed herself. She had a cloth shopping bag and something in it. She was just beginning to think that nothing would happen when she saw first Jenn and then Belonwu. She saw Jenn react to the person of interest, saw her make a phone call as she kept walking, and as both the detective and the suspect went out of sight onto the larger street, Emily got out and locked her car. She took her shopping bag along.

 Belonwu kept on to the big intersection with Washtenaw Avenue, crossed, and retraced his semi-clandestine path of the night before. Jenn followed, still talking to dispatch. Before, she'd just been looking for help with a possible interview. Now, she had a suspect in potential flight, carrying luggage, and he was heading into the heart of Art Fair. This was a bit more important-sounding, and the dispatcher was trying to get into contact with officers on foot patrol or with the UM police. Jenn kept reporting their locations as she followed Belonwu onto campus and toward the diag.

MacArthur was indulging himself that morning. For a number of years, he'd made a point of getting up early on Art Fair's opening day and messing with it. He'd put on a hat and sunscreen and good walking shoes, and lately, he'd take his handicapped-parking tag along. He'd park somewhere near the Fair, open the small doors to the back seat area of his truck, and unleash the dogs of war. Snacker, originally, and now Goose as well were Mac's secret weapons in the struggle against tourists with strollers. In heavy pedestrian traffic, the only thing more inconvenient and annoying than a double-wide baby carriage would have to be a pair of large, friendly dogs on leashes. He took a great and perverse pride in demonstrating that he could keep two four-footed creatures under control and out of other people's personal space, whereas Mom couldn't control a four-wheeled vehicle, even when all you had to do was push it. He had a whole repertoire of snarky comments, things like "I got licenses for these guys. You got one for that thing?" He could be quite a jerk when he wanted to be.

Belonwu walked along the main diagonal sidewalk until it crossed a lateral path. He turned left and as he did so, he glanced back quickly. There were a couple of young people going the other way, and an older woman in more businesslike clothes. Nothing seemed ominous, and he kept going toward State Street, teeming with vendors and pedestrian traffic. He turned right, walking behind the booths, and noticed the woman again. He'd never seen her, but she'd made the same turn he had; in his mind, anyone wearing anything more than shorts in weather like this was suspect. He walked faster, and turned between two stalls, merging into the foot traffic.

The 'older woman', of course, was Jenn Langton, and she told the dispatcher that she'd lost contact with her suspect. She started to run toward State, jogging, trying not to look like she was pursuing someone.

Belonwu couldn't have run if he'd wanted to, since the street was clogged with people moving slowly, stopping to examine merchandise, stopping to converse. He angled left, moving away from the flow of humanity, and as he came out between two booths, he found himself at the corner of William, the route he'd planned to take down to the Bus Station. It was clogged with vendors and booths, too, but he turned anyway. In front of him, people parted and he stepped into an open space, right in the middle of the street and about eight feet across. Facing him at the other end of it was the cause of the opening, a short man with a pair of excited, intense dogs: Mac MacArthur!

The initial mental processes of all parties, the two humans and the two dogs, were diverse. Mac saw only a young man with luggage coming out of the crowd. He'd seen Belonwu's picture, but it didn't register instantly. The dogs thought nothing much about Belonwu at all; they were absorbed with the fantastic smells from restaurants and food carts. For them, Art

Fair was an olfactory psychedelia, layer upon layer of meaning, most of it having to do with things edible. Belonwu was the first one to assess the situation tactically. He recognized Mac and he recognized the dogs, and his assessment was quick and prejudicial, even if wrong. He was caught! The woman behind *was* following him, there must be cops in the crowd, and here, blocking his path, was the shadowy spook and his demonic dogs!

Oh! My! God! He went from plan A through plans M or N in a matter of a second, and he arrived at the last and only remaining plan on his list.

He was armed, to a certain extent. The small gun he had in a pants pocket was in keeping with his Victorian persona, and he was only carrying it in order to dispose of it easily before having to board a plane. It was a reproduction of a .41 caliber derringer, made in Italy. It was not an assault rifle, a machine gun, a thermonuclear device, or anything else a modern cop might reasonably expect to encounter. It was a gun, yes, but only technically. It had a percussion lock and it was loaded with a single shot's worth of black powder and a round lead ball. At anything more than a few feet, it was wildly inaccurate, but it was all he had, and he was only a few feet from his target, anyway. He drew the pistol, cocked it, and pointed it at Mac.

MacArthur's mind was working to grasp the meaning of the tableau; a man who looked like a second string college athlete had dropped his luggage and was pointing a John Wilkes Booth derringer at him. His own right hand was mysteriously freed up, because the leash he'd been holding with it had vanished. People who'd noticed the little gun were screaming and pushing to get away. And then the gun went off.

The ball left the barrel, closely followed by a small group of sparks and a large gray cloud of smoke. It flew forward and hit Mac squarely on the left breast. It bounced off. Belonwu had purchased the derringer at a gun show, second hand and without any kind of instructions. He'd guessed at the correct amount of powder, loaded it, and never gotten around to firing it. His guess at the load had been short by seventy-five percent or more.

Mac was still operating on impressions and reflex. His left hand was involved with Snacker's leash, since she was averse to loud noises and was trying to hide behind him. His right hand was free because Goose was half way to Belonwu, roaring as he went. Mac realized suddenly "He shot me!" and fumbled under his over shirt for his sidearm. Distantly, he was aware of the crowd panicking at the noise, the smoke, and the dog.

Belonwu himself was seized with panic and horror. It didn't occur to him to do anything more than turn away from Goose, and he'd gotten halfway through that move when he was tackled from the right. Jenn Langton had elbowed her way through the shoppers, seen Belonwu shoot, and lunged into him. Unfortunately, he was large and she wasn't, and he didn't go down. Rather, he swung on around to the right, swinging her with him, and tried to break away. At that moment, Goose latched onto his left arm. He yelled with pain and tried to turn back, Jenn still clinging to him. As he tried to get free of the dog and the detective, both intent on his destruction, a third force appeared on the scene. Emily Weiden stepped out of the crowd and slammed him in the side of the head with her canvas bag. His vision sparked and then darkened. His knees buckled, and he fell, landing partly on Goose. Emily stepped back; when she'd left her apartment that morning, she'd picked up the bag and loaded it with the heaviest and most dense object she had, a hardbound copy of the complete Goethe.

By now, Snacker had seen enough, peeking through Mac's legs, to realize that Goose and a lady she recognized were embroiled with someone, and since her friends were attacking him, he must be someone who needed to be attacked. The big noise was over, and her fear vanished. She rushed forward, dragging Mac along, and joined the fracas. Mac, for his part, decided against drawing his little Glock and instead yanked his retiree badge off his belt, holding it up and shouting "Police!" loudly. It was all he could think of to say; even if he'd known what was going on, an explanation of it wouldn't have been something one could shout at a terrified group of tourists and soccer moms.

Oddly, most of the crowd did the sensible thing. Somebody had fired off a gun; somebody was on the ground, being eaten by dogs; a guy who looked nothing at all like a cop was waving a badge around and shouting.

The majority of the bystanders kept right on pushing outward from the scene, trying to distance themselves from whatever horror was taking place. The impetus to withdraw was increased by two Ann Arbor patrol officers, pushing their way in and also shouting "Police! Police!" A cook from one of the food stands showed up with a chef's knife, thinking he might be needed, but he changed his mind and faded back into the multitude. So did Emily.

It took a while to disentangle the fighters, corral the dogs, and get the unconscious Belonwu handcuffed. It took longer to get patrol cars and an ambulance through the Fair. It took even longer than that for Mac to realize that he was slightly sore where the bullet hit him. He pulled up his T-shirt and saw only a red mark, something that would probably become a bruise.

Jenn noticed. "Christ, Mac! Are you okay?"

"Oh, yeah, I guess. It's about par for the course for Art Fair."

... its melancholy, long, withdrawing roar ...

On Wednesday afternoon, Jenn finally got sufficiently free of the crime scene details to check voicemail. She flipped quickly through the list of calls, and she saw with pleasure a message from Andy Patel. It was Andy's usual: "Got a couple of things. Give me a call."

"Hi, Jenn. Thanks for the call back."

"It's been a little crazy. Sorry it took me a while."

"Oh, no problem. Actually, I've got two things. One social, one, ah, professional."

"Okay," she said, "How about the social one first?" She'd had enough professional issues for one day, really.

"So I was talking to one of the guys here. The only one I'd trust on the topic of food. And he said there's a barbeque place down in Greektown that's actually good."

"Barbeque? Wonderful! I don't think tonight would work, though." She had an astonishing amount to do, yet, cleaning up this absurd mess. A chase through Art Fair, a shooting, civilian dogs helping take down a suspect; she tried to remember a term Andy's old partner at the FBI had used. Cluster-something.

"Yeah, I think we'd be better off waiting for the weekend," Andy said. "Which would be better? Friday or Saturday?"

"Let's call it Saturday."

"Great! We could meet at my place and take one car."

"Can't wait," she said. "Now, what's the professional thing?"

"Well, this may not be any use, but I thought I'd pass it along. We put a watch on the Mbanugo name ... the old guy ... to see if there were any airline purchases or big withdrawals and so on. Useless. I mean, he's in bed, he's not going anywhere. But it's routine. Anyway, we got a hit, not on him but on your suspect. Belonwu. "

"You did?"

"Yeah, we did. He's got a ticket to Nigeria! Their embassy issued him a visa. The whole deal. He's going tomorrow, out of Chicago."

Jenn stared at the phone.

"Ah, Andy," she said. "I know all that. I've got his boarding pass right here."

"What?"

"Haven't you seen any news?"

Andy was stumped. He hadn't seen anything, hadn't been outside the office, in fact.

"So you arrested him?"

"You could say that. Do a search on 'art fair shooting'. Go ahead."

"All right, hold on." There was a pause. "Holy ... are you kidding me?"

"Nope. We got him. Not without a fight, though."

"Jenn! Is that you in the pictures, wrestling with the kid? Where did the dogs come from?"

"That's me. Those are Mac's dogs. It's a long story. Oh, and one of our informants was apparently stalking him, too. Hit him over the head with a book bag or something and just walked away."

"But it says here ... 'A retired detective was hit ...' He shot MacArthur?"

"Um, technically. He had this little antique gun, and Mac just got a bruise out of it."

"Lord!"

"Look, I've got to dig back into this mess. The good news: we got the grandson. The bad news: until he wakes up and decides to tell us about it, we still don't know why in hell he killed the professor. Or if he did, I guess. I'm just a little bit tired ..."

"Sure. I'll let you go. But give me a call again when you can. I want to hear this whole thing. How do you get into these weird cases?" The only other murder Jenn had ever handled got Andy into a firefight. He remembered it very, very clearly.

"We don't get all that many, up here," she said. "I suppose I'm just lucky."

"Or something. Well, call me, and we'll figure out Saturday."

"You bet. Barbeque! Yum! Talk to you later, *cher*." Jenn hung up.

Andy set his phone down. The story was hugely interesting, of course, and enough so that he didn't consider until much later Jenn's faux-Cajun signoff. *She called me* cher, he thought, a full day later.

Jerry Mbanugo suddenly opened his eyes. He struggled to sit up. One of the medications he'd been taking was a sort of sedative, but in the quantities they were giving him, it was producing hallucinations; he was in a stark white hospital room, but he saw the walls as intricate carvings, something like twisted tree limbs in dark old wood, colored by smoke and softened by years of hands. They were alive, winding around each other, and periodically a flattened human form would take part, like a king from an Assyrian relief, bearded and wearing a helmet. He tried to touch the walls, but they stayed out of reach. A hand seemed to be squeezing Jerry's chest, his breathing was difficult, and the visions began to darken and slide away.

Katherine had been dozing in a chair beside the bed. She woke up and reached for his hand. He looked hard at the last faint, dissolving Assyrian. "I apologize," he said, and he slowly lay back down.

The nurses straightened him out in the bed and took the IV out of his arm. They left Katherine with him for a few minutes. Phone calls were made, routine steps were taken.

Days later on, Jenn and Larry Whitaker were in Katherine Mbanugo's living room, trying to make some sense out of the case. They'd expressed their sympathy for Jerry's death, and they'd gone through the motions of, "We want to help your grandson ..." All that aside, though, they were talking to a relative of a man in jail, charged with murder. It was bound to be awkward.

"Mrs. Mbanugo," Jenn said, "What we need to know is how your family connects to Professor Kirk."

"That's the man you say Belonwu killed, right?"

"Yes."

"I never heard of him. Not until the news stories about the boy bein' arrested."

"But you met him, didn't you?" asked Larry. "When he came to see your husband?"

168

"He never came here. You mean, this Kirk guy? He never came to see Jerry."

"Are you sure?" said Jenn.

"Yeah, I'm sure. Jerry was in bed. He couldn't get up. I was here all the time or one of the family was. Nobody came to see him except the kids and the grandkids."

"But Belonwu says your husband talked to him. He says he told him things."

"What kind of things?"

"Things about Nigeria, about what he did back there."

"No, no. He couldn't have. Nobody came to see him. I'd know."

"Well, how about on the phone, then?" said Larry.

"No phone in his bedroom. If he got calls, I'd have to take a message. Nobody called him, anyway."

"Letters? On the net, maybe?"

"He didn't use a computer. I'd have to do it for him. And letters, I'd have to mail 'em. I'd know."

"So let me make sure I understand," said Jenn. "Mr. Mbanugo never talked to Doctor Kirk, as far as you know? Or anybody else, about Nigeria?"

"Jerry was sick the last two or three years. Really sick. I had to look after him all the time. He was fading away, you know? At the end, he'd say things to *me* that didn't make any sense. Even if there was somebody I don't know about, Jerry couldn't have told 'em anything. Can I talk to the boy? I'd like to hear what he thinks he was doing, killin' that man."

"We aren't going assume anything, and you shouldn't either, Mrs. Mbanugo," said Jenn. "He hasn't been convicted yet." "*Oh, but he will be,*" she thought. The things in his workshop at the parents' house, the black powder residue in his car, the near confession he'd given them: no real doubt that he did it. But *why* was still a mystery, and there were limits on what Belonwu would say. He was sorry he'd had to kill the man, sorry he'd shot at MacArthur. He seemed to think the CIA was involved somehow, but as soon as that subject came up, he'd just say, "I can't discuss that." The best they could get to was that Belonwu believed Jerry had told Kirk something, and that had caused him to commit a bizarre and improbable murder and plan a flight to Nigeria. It all had something to do with Kirk, but now Katherine's very credible-sounding story seemed to deny any connection with Kirk at all. They'd found a copy of Kirk's letter to Jerry, but now it looked as though the two had never met, talked, exchanged secrets of any kind, let alone those worth dying for.

Katherine glanced out the window. "Here comes my granddaughter," she said. "Are we done? I've got to talk to her. She's had a lot of loss right now."

"All right," said Jenn. "We'll get out of your way. If we need anything else, we'll call you."

Akunna came in as the detectives were leaving. She looked slightly pregnant, tired, distraught. Her eyes were red, and she seemed not all that far from tears. She and Katherine exchanged a long hug.

"This is my granddaughter," said Katherine.

"How do you do," said Jenn. "I know this must be hard for you, your grandfather passing and your brother, ah, in trouble."

"That's not all," said Katherine. "Her husband's missing, too."

Midday: Belonwu Mbanugo lay awake on a bunk in his cell. He stared straight up at the ceiling, willing his mind to stay idle, to think nothing at all. Specifically, he tried to suppress what he'd just been told: his grandfather probably never told Kirk anything, let alone about the diamonds. He shut his eyes tightly, clinched his jaw, tried to force the thoughts away. He was only partly successful; he allowed himself to think, *I wish I had a bigger bed.*

Late evening: Colleen was upstairs, getting ready to turn in. Mac shut off the downstairs lights and stumped up to his office. He powered down the computer, turned off the desk lamp and the overhead, and stepped back out into the hall. Colleen came out of the bathroom and then stopped in the bedroom door. Mac looked over her shoulder. The MacArthurs had a king size bed and mattress, and now it was occupied by a pair of king size dogs, sprawled in such a way as to take up the entire thing.

Coleen said, "We're going to need a bigger bed."

Early morning: Jenn woke up, and her brain immediately ran its set of start-up scripts. "*What time is it? What day is it? Is it a work day? What do I need to get done?*" Some mornings, she was calm, grateful for sleep but ready to put it aside. On others, she woke up worrying; an anxiety or some unmet responsibility would be instantly on the table. It might be a professional topic, or it might be something from her personal life; something in the house needed to be fixed or cleaned, one of the daughters might be in trouble again, something had to be purchased or returned or paid for. On those days, the amount of time it took to get out of bed would be determined by when two curves crossed, the plotted values of avoidance (most of her worries weren't things she could handle while she was still in bed) and guilt (the longer she stayed in bed, the less time to put out fires.)

This morning seemed to be unfolding along a new, third path. She stretched and yawned, extending her left arm. The elbow bumped Andy Patel on the side of his head. He made a semi-conscious noise and rolled over toward her. His eyes opened, and he smiled.

"Damn it, Patel," Jenn said, "One of us is going to have to get a bigger bed."

"*One thing about Greece*," thought Achilles Gordon; "*no matter how bad the economy gets, the sun still shines.*" It was a beautiful morning as he went through customs. Eleftherios Venizelos airport was still clean and prosperous-looking. "Good morning," he said, handing over his passport.

"Good morning, sir," said the agent. He flipped through the pages and with a smile, returned it. "Welcome back!"

Not far from Detroit's downtown, three miles out along Gratiot Avenue, there's one of America's most startling artifacts of failure. The Packard Plant, a vast complex crammed into a strip one block wide by eight or nine long, rose at the beginning of the twentieth century, and it turned out cars for more than fifty years. After Packard and then Studebaker-Packard withered away, the plant closed as a plant, but it was still occupied by other businesses through the nineties. After that, the three-and-a-half-million square feet of industrial space became a rapidly decaying symbol of economic disaster. Unlike the infamous Michigan Central Station, the Packard Plant isn't a photographic icon. Instead of looking like a ruin of a bygone civilization, it looks like a war relic, a place that was bombed and abandoned. Photos and satellite imagery remind you of Berlin or of London's Docklands, circa 1945.

Few living things inhabit the plant now. There are a few courageous or desperate homeless people; weeds and junk trees; mice and rats; and man's usual close neighbor, raccoons. Raccoons are clever, if not especially intelligent. They follow routine and, we can assume, are capable of feeling certain moods: anger, pleasure, fear, and, maybe, annoyance. One of the larger members of the species lived near the plant entrance, and for the last month, he'd been regularly annoyed. His favorite path had been disrupted as it went from his den to a place where water collected, where he could reliably get a drink. It had been a smooth, covered, safe route; now it was partly blocked by roofing material that had been moved around. As he scurried toward the water hole, he now had to go around the pile of refuse and climb over a human leg, sticking out from under it. The foot had no shoe, but it still wore a dress sock, and the leg was still covered in dark trousers that might have been part of a two-for-one suit. The rest of Charlie Blake was under the junk pile, waiting to complete its return to mother earth.

Enugu, the capitol of Enugu State, is a city of *face-me-I-face-you* flats, squares of small homes that face inward, making a central courtyard. The coal mines are nearly played out, and strangely enough, the city is becoming something of a film-making center. Not far from Saint Bartholomew's, there's an open area, created a few months before to allow a vegetable market some space to grow. The bulldozers had left it a flat, unpaved field, open to the wind. On a dusty afternoon, two women were standing beside a dozen baskets of produce, arguing in a pro forma way over prices. The ground the goods rested on was where Jerry's safe house had been.

... the moon lies fair ...

Mac's phone made the diminuendo chiming sound that meant a text message had arrived. Colleen was letting him know that she'd be late getting home. Would he give the dogs a quick walk around the block? It had rained briefly, an hour ago, but the sun was back out, and Mac was happy for an excuse to wander around in the spring weather. He changed into his waterproof shoes. Snacker and Goose noted what he was doing and came to help. Obviously, one of their humans, sitting on the lower steps of the stairs, struggling with shoes and cursing, was both signaling that a walk was coming up and was in need of their assistance and encouragement. Mac had to abandon the shoes for a minute and rub two sets of ears before the dogs would get their noses out of his face and let him finish tying the laces.

Walks were always fine with the Shepherds, unless it was blazingly hot or pouring rain. Snow was no deterrent, nor was mud, although Snacker would delicately side-step puddles unless she was in pursuit of something. Both understood and accepted leashes; they would rather have run loose, but except at the dog park, that wasn't in the cards and they knew it. They were also accommodating and adaptable. They matched their gait and agenda to the human with them, trotting along at a good pace with Colleen, slowing down and investigating things with Mac. When they went out with Colleen, she was giving them a walk; with Mac, they were mostly walking him.

Mac hooked them up to their leashes, put on a broad-brimmed hat (in case it rained again; he hated rain on his head), and stocked his treat bag with a mix of biscuits and leftover chicken, chopped up into bite-size snacks. He eased the group out the front door, and the dogs waited politely while he fumbled out his keys and locked the dead bolt. Then they headed down a short path to the street and a sharp left turn. Goose walked more or less in a straight line, Snacker moved in shorter vectors, surfing the canine web at strategically placed trees and a fire hydrant.

Then, as had happened many times before, she froze. Her tail came up, her ears went forward, and everything about her body language indicated a laser-like focus. Ahead twenty-five feet or so was a rabbit or actually an *ersatz* rabbit, made of painted concrete and set in place to decorate a neighbor's yard. With her aging eyesight, Snacker often mistook the symbol for the actuality, no matter how many times she'd seen it, and tonight she stalked slowly toward it, lowering her head. Goose reacted only momentarily; he knew how it would all end, and he just went along with the charade, doing the dog equivalent of rolling his eyes. At ten feet or so, Snacker suddenly dropped all signs of interest, recognizing the lawn ornament for what it was. She veered off, tucking her paws into her pockets and whistling (figuratively speaking). Everything about her said 'I meant to do that'.

On the second floor of the rabbit's house, the owner opened a window and greeted the team. "Fooled her again," he yelled.

"I'm glad it *isn't* alive," Mac shouted back. "One of these days, there'll be a real rabbit, and then God help me."

"Where's Colleen?"

"Working late ... later than usual, anyway."

"You get the grill going yet?" Most houses in this little urban enclave had a propane grill in the back yard or at least a kettle for charcoal.

"Absolutely! Did the usual chicken last night, in fact. How about you?"

"Not yet ... maybe this weekend."

The Shepherds were willing to put up with a certain amount of human dialogue on their walks, but the key phrase was *their walks*. They'd been standing patiently, but Mac could sense that patience wearing thin. He signed off.

"Enjoy the weather. Come on, guys." The three of them went on their way, following their usual route along residential streets and through a vast grade school playground. They ducked through a gap in a fence, walked between a church and an apartment building, and pointed their respective noses south along Packard and toward home. Something along the way made MacArthur think of dreams.

Dreams. What a strange nightmare this Kirk business had been. He'd visited Belonwu and tried to find out what it was about; the young man would go just so far and no farther. He told Mac that it was becoming a dream already, one in which his own thoughts and attitudes were slipping away. He said that he couldn't remember the reasons for some of the things he'd done.

Dreams. Mac pictured the subconscious as a twisted, unconstrained version of your conscious mind, running through fantasy patterns and flavored with a few of your more prominent anxieties. They might be upsetting or frustrating, even frightening, but they weren't often pathological. No, your own dreams weren't likely to be dangerous. Other people's dreams, though, that could be a different story. Other people's dreams could kill you.

===

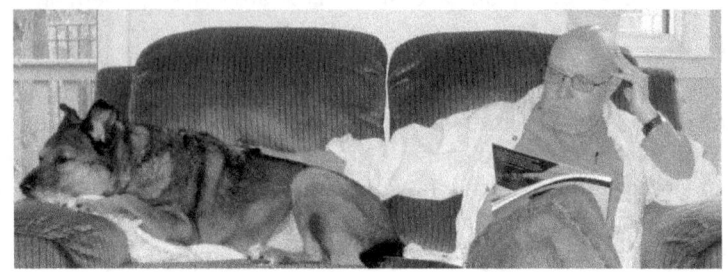

Joseph McConnell describes himself as a retired technical bureaucrat. In and around his day jobs, he's been writing for decades, once sharing the cover of Whole Earth Review with Allen Ginsberg. Born in (extremely) rural Michigan, he's lived in Ann Arbor since 1977 and—whether the city is prepared to admit it or not—considers himself a stakeholder. **Clash by Night** *is his second novel.*

Other books by Joseph McConnell:

Many Believable Lies

The Least Weasel

www.ingramcontent.com/pod-product-compliance
Lightning Source LLC
Chambersburg PA
CBHW070920130626
46555CB00001B/220